BETTER LATE THAN NEVER

LAURYN ALEXANDER

CLOVER RIDGE PRES

ONE

"One more question before our time is up." Cassandra Kelly, the anchor of *Miami Today*, a local morning news/magazine show, slid a quick glance at the card in her lap, then smiled her trademark smile at her guest.

Relief washed over Lisa McKenzie. *One more question. She could do this.* Although her television debut hadn't been nearly as terrifying as she'd expected it to be, she was well aware it was because of the skill and talent of the young woman sitting in the chair facing her.

It's almost over. Lisa was confident she hadn't said or done anything to humiliate either herself or Randolph Plaza, the exclusive boutique hotel in downtown Miami where she worked. That was all she'd prayed for when Devon Randolph III, the owner of the Randolph chain of boutique hotels and her future father-in-law, had suggested—strongly—that she appear on the show.

Struggling to overcome the negative publicity the hotel had been subjected to lately by the local media, he was convinced that Lisa's fresh, innocent smile would be enough to ward off speculation that the hotel was on the brink of financial ruin.

Cassandra shifted her position, only a few inches but enough to make it seem as if she and Lisa were best friends about to share a secret. "Rumors are circulating that the construction costs for the new hotel are drastically over budget. And our sources tell us that there is a serious cash flow problem because of inferior materials, delays and shoddy workmanship. Do you have any comment?"

Lisa wasn't surprised by the question. She was only surprised that it had taken almost the whole interview for Cassandra to confront her about the company's finances. She considered the question for a moment, recalling the short press release she'd prepared and memorized the evening before.

The Randolph organization *was* in serious financial trouble. The estimates for the new hotel being built at the airport had been drastically underestimated, and the recession in the economy had forced several of their major clients to either cancel or downsize the conferences the hotel relied on as a major source of revenue. That, plus the fact that people weren't traveling the way they used to, especially the kind of people who stayed at the Randolph chain, had seriously affected the company's bottom line.

But she certainly wasn't going to admit any of that on national television.

Her voice was soft and controlled when she finally responded. "Unfortunately," she began, smiling into the camera, "inflation has caused construction costs to skyrocket since the original figures were announced. But I can assure you that the financial status of the Randolph organization is completely secure."

Her glance slid to the monitor at the side of the set. The camera had switched back to Cassandra.

"We're pleased to hear that," she said.

Lisa wondered if the flicker of disappointment flitting across the woman's face was a figment of her imagination or if Cassandra had been hoping Lisa would let something newsworthy slip out.

The red light switched from one camera to another. Well," Cassandra continued, changing her position back to face the camera with a smile, "that's all the time we have for this morning. My guest has been Lisa McKenzie, assistant manager of the Randolph Plaza, and soon to be Mrs. Carter Randolph."

She turned to Lisa with a friendly grin. "Thanks for joining me this morning, and once again, our sincerest congratulations on your engagement. I hope you'll both be very happy."

To the camera, she added her sign-off, "Don't forget, we live in a first-class city. So get out there and enjoy..." She paused for effect, then added, "...Miami Today." She held the smile until a voice behind the studio lights shouted, "We're clear!"

Lisa hadn't realized she'd been holding her breath until she heard the stage manager's words. An audible sigh escaped her lips and she leaned back in the beige armchair, thankful that the ordeal was finally over. She glanced at the clock on the wall just out of camera range. It had only been ten minutes, but without question, it had been the longest ten minutes of her life.

"You were absolutely wonderful," Cassandra gushed as one of the stagehands rushed over to remove the microphone clip from Lisa's jacket. "Look at that," she said, pointing to the monitor. Lisa's face filled the screen. "The camera loves you."

The face looking back at Lisa was so unlike her that she barely recognized herself. She chuckled. She did look good, she supposed, but that only proved that proper lighting and the right make-up could transform Cinderella into a princess. "The camera may love me, but the next time I plan to be on film is when I'm walking down the aisle."

She checked the time again. "I'm sorry, but I really have to run," she said, getting up and smoothing out a wrinkle in her gray wool skirt. "With the official opening of the new hotel less than two weeks away, there are a thousand little details to take care of."

"Of course. I understand. I do appreciate you taking the time to appear on the show," Cassandra replied. "Perhaps you'll come back again after the wedding and tell us what it's like to be married to one of the city's sexiest men."

Not a chance, Lisa said. With a grin and a quick wave, Lisa turned and hurried out of the building.

Jack Brennan hummed to himself as he slid the razor over his chin. Life was good. Or as good as it was ever going to get. A new penthouse condo overlooking Biscayne Bay, a cozy beach house on Sandpiper Key, a successful business. What more could a man want? Nothing, right?

So why did he have a nagging sense of unease, of confusion, a feeling that something vital was missing from his life. Was it because his thirtieth birthday was approaching, and his life hadn't turned out the way he'd expected it to? In most ways, he'd achieved more than he'd ever dreamed. And without his family's money, too, he reminded himself. He was proud of that. He had every reason to be.

But by now he'd assumed he'd have the house in the suburbs, the wife waiting for him at night, and the 2.5 kids the statistics told him he would have. There was no way any of that was going to happen in the near future, though.

Get over it! There's at least a dozen guys I know who'd kill to be in my shoes. Free, no ties.

Clearing his mind from the disturbing thoughts crowding his brain, he wiped a few small globs of shaving cream off his face with a facecloth, shook a few drops of aftershave into his hands and slapped his cheeks with the liquid. His skin tingled.

The muted voices of an early morning television show met his ears as he turned off the faucet. He dried his hands on the towel hanging on the hook behind the door and headed into the bedroom. In the corner of the room, a giant flat-screen TV was set to one of the local channels.

Now where did I leave my sneakers, he wondered, scanning the cluttered bedroom for his well-worn Reeboks. There was no sign of them. He crouched down and lifted the corner of the down-filled comforter off the plush carpet. There they were, under the bed behind one of his socks. He dragged them out and then perched on the side of the bed to put them on.

He was lacing up the right shoe when he heard the voice. He froze. He hadn't heard that voice in almost twelve years, but he would know it anywhere.

His eyes shot to the TV. Lisa's face filled the screen, much as it had filled his dreams far too often, for far too many years.

He'd searched for her for so long before he'd given up and let the past die. And now, here she was, almost right under his nose.

"Man, she looks good," he muttered out loud as the picture faded and a small boy gobbling down cereal appeared on the screen. She'd changed. Now, instead of the cute and bubbly girl with the huge glasses he remembered, she was a sophisticated, beautiful woman. The chestnut-colored hair that he remem-bered hanging down her back or braided into a pigtail had been feathered into a halo around her pixie-shaped face. Her hazel eyes, contoured and enhanced with just the right shades of eye shadow and mascara, sparkled with humor at an amusing comment from the hostess of the show. Soft pink lipstick and a sweep of blush gave her a healthy glow.

He sat, transfixed, waiting. It seemed like forever before the show came back on. His eyes were riveted to the screen. A shadow of a smile crossed his face as the hostess's voice welcomed the viewers back and posed the next question to Lisa. He stared, mesmerized, as she answered the questions put to her, calmly, logically, without actually offering any information. Those years on the debate team in high school hadn't been wasted after all.

She still had it. She'd always been good at dodging issues and changing the subject whenever she was uncomfortable. During their senior year, he'd even suggested that she go into politics or law. She was a natural.

The hostess was speaking again, and Jack caught the words 'assistant manager of Randolph Place'.

The Randolph. Only a few blocks away. And she was almost top dog. How about that? Not that he was really surprised. He'd always figured she'd go places, even when she'd assured him she'd be happy with a house in the country and a whole boatload of kids.

Congratulations... Engagement... What was this woman talking about?

The words spun crazily in Jack's head. Congratulations...engagement...Carter Randolph. It couldn't be. Lisa couldn't be engaged to be married. And to one of the Randolphs, of all people. The credits began to roll and the screen faded into darkness.

Jack stared blankly at the TV as the theme song from *The Flintstones* filled the room and Fred Flintstone slid down a dinosaur's back into his car, then sped away. But Jack saw only Lisa's face.

More than a dozen years ago, he'd given his heart to the woman behind that face. And now, he realized that she quite probably still had it firmly in her hands.

Getting married...getting married... He couldn't get the words out of his mind.

He had to stop this wedding, he thought as he bounded up and began to pace. She couldn't get married. If she knew the truth...

He paused in mid-stride. She must know, right? Otherwise she wouldn't be getting married. But if she didn't…she'd find out soon enough.

He'd done everything he could to fix things, hadn't he? She was the one who'd changed her cell phone number and whose family had disappeared from their home town without even having the decency to let anyone know where they were going. He'd searched for her on social media, but jeez, there were thousands of McKenzies on Facebook and Twitter. Yeah, he reasoned, he'd done everything he could.

If she didn't know, it wasn't his fault. She should have done her own due diligence, shouldn't she? Then again, he hadn't found out through due diligence. It had been a fluke, a coincidence. Nothing more.

And why should he even care if she knew the truth about what had happened?

He couldn't answer his own question. He didn't know why he should care. He only knew that he did. He cared far too much.

This wedding was wrong. He was sure of it. He'd

met the Randolphs a couple of times, and that was all it had taken to figure out what kind of people they were. Lisa wouldn't be happy with them. Lisa with her over-sized sweaters and cutoff jeans. Lisa on third base on her softball team. Lisa playing with the spaniel puppy that her father had given her just before he was killed...

She could have changed, he supposed, but he had a gut feeling that she couldn't have changed that much. She didn't belong at charity balls and hosting teas for the matrons of society. She was a donut and muffin kind of girl, not hors oeuvres and canapés.

Besides, Lisa should be with him. The realization struck him with the force of a hammer. She was the wife he'd expected to have, and she was supposed to be the mother of their 2.5 children. They should be living in their picket-fenced bungalow in the suburbs or the house at the beach with a golden retriever or two that they'd talked about. It might have been eleven years, four months and sixteen days, but he hadn't changed. Somehow, he had to make her see that she belonged with him, not with Carter Randolph.

But how could he stop her? There was nothing he could do to prevent her from going ahead with the wedding. He couldn't exactly walk back into her life after all these years like they were nineteen years old again and ask her not to marry Carter.

Could he?

"Hawaii would be a perfect spot for our honeymoon, don't you think?" Lisa tucked her feet under her on the couch in Carter Randolph's office and flipped to the next page of the travel brochure. "Unless you'd rather go to Europe?" She glanced up. "Carter?"

"Sorry. What did you say?" Carter looked up from the pile of computer printouts on his desk.

"Hawaii or Europe?"

"Whatever you like," he replied absently, his attention already back on the columns of figures on the paper.

She put the brochure on a table and took a bite out of the tuna sandwich she'd had sent up from the hotel kitchen. When she was finished, she wiped her fingers on a linen napkin and got up. She crossed the room, stopping behind Carter's chair. He was sitting at a large oak desk, folders and papers covering every available inch of the surface. Gently, she rested her hands on either side of his neck and began to knead the knots of tension in his shoulders. "Maybe we should leave a decision on the honeymoon until later," she said softly. "You seem to have other things on your mind right now."

Carter glanced up at her, revealing the dazzling smile that made him one of the city's sexiest men, a label he'd been given the year before. The smile reached his grey eyes, and smoothed the frown lines rutting his forehead. He was an exceptionally good-looking man, GQ personified, and she often felt she was having a dream and soon someone would pinch her and she would wake up. He was one of the city's most eligible bachelors, and over the years, he'd been linked with some of the most beautiful and wealthiest women in the country. Yet he'd chosen her to be his wife. She had no idea why he preferred her to them, but she was glad he had, and she had no intention of questioning his choice.

Carter raked his hands through his thick, black hair and sighed. "Actually, darling, I hate to disappoint you, but I think it's impossible to take time for a honeymoon right now. With the way things are..." He sighed, letting the words fade away, and Lisa noticed for the first time the tiny lines of fatigue registering on his face.

Carter was under so much pressure at the moment that she almost felt guilty even mentioning their honeymoon, but she was sure that that was exactly what he needed—to get away, relax and enjoy himself.

She didn't want to be a widow before she'd really had a chance to be a wife, and the way he was pushing himself, she was convinced he was heading for a heart attack, even if he was only in his mid-thirties. She'd heard just the week before about a man in his twenties who'd suffered a heart attack they'd put down to stress. He'd died.

"You're exhausted," she pointed out, "and you need a vacation. You've been working so hard lately that we've hardly had a minute to spend together."

Carter smiled softly and patted her hand. "And you worry far too much about me."

Lisa glanced at the papers on the desk. "Is it that serious?"

Carter nodded. "I'm afraid so."

"But surely your father and your brother can handle things for a couple of weeks. We won't be leaving until the hotel is fully functional and all the bugs are ironed out."

"I'm sorry, darling," he explained. "This is a very delicate situation. If it isn't handled properly, it could be devastating for the future of the entire company. And consequently our future. I've discussed it with Father and James, and they'd prefer that I stay until we're back on firm footing again. I'm sure that eventually, things will straighten out. But in the meantime, I don't think it would be wise to go out of the country. I need to be here to keep my eye on what's going on on a day-to-day basis."

Her hands rested on his shoulders. "I understand," she said. And she did. She didn't like what she was hearing, but she did know how important it was to him to be in control of the situation. He couldn't do that from thousands of miles away, even with email and Zoom meetings.

But she couldn't give up just yet, even though she knew she was beginning to sound a little churlish, even to her own ears. "But Carter, we've been planning this wedding for a year now."

Okay, she admitted grudgingly, she did sound like a spoiled brat. She was being selfish, a little. She wanted a honeymoon. Every bride wanted that though, didn't they? Was it too much to ask that they spend a couple of weeks alone, without the constant pressure of work and the family to interrupt? But it wasn't just for her. She was thinking of him, too.

Randolph's, the small chain of exclusive hotels owned by Carter's family, was a huge responsibility. And Carter took that responsibility very seriously. She understood that. It was one of the qualities that she most admired in him.

But to give up her honeymoon... Her honeymoon was a special time she'd dreamed of since she was a little girl.

"I don't think I'm being unreasonable because I want to spend some time some time—alone—with my new husband," she grumbled.

Carter sighed, then reached up and squeezed her hand gently before he turned his attention back to the sheaf of papers on his desk. "I'm sorry," he murmured absently, his finger following the line of figures on the document in front of him.

She opened her mouth to respond, then changed her mind.

As if he sensed she wasn't satisfied with his apology, he looked up at her. "Believe me, I want to spend time with you, too," he said. "Perhaps we can manage a few days over a weekend, since you have your heart set on it. What about the mountains? We could rent a little cabin and be completely isolated from the outside world. How does that sound?"

A weekend. A few days. That was all the time he was prepared to spend away from business. Oh well, a few days was better than nothing, she supposed, trying to quell her disappointment.

After all, it didn't really matter where they spent their first days together as man and wife. The important thing was that they would be together.

They probably wouldn't be spending much time out of their room anyway, not if the last few weeks were any indication. It was becoming more and more difficult to keep Carter's advances in check, and he'd jokingly warned her more than once that when the wedding was over and they were husband and wife, he intended to make up for all the times she'd pushed him away.

"All right. The mountains it is. We can discuss the details later, then," Lisa suggested with a resigned smile. "But Hawaii in the spring."

Carter returned her smile, raising her hand from his shoulder to his lips. "Hawaii in the spring. Definitely."

He stood up and slid his arms around Lisa's waist.

She rested her head on his shoulder and closed her eyes. She sensed rather than felt Carter's lips on her cheek. She pulled away from his embrace and raised her eyes to meet his.

"Meanwhile, back to work," Lisa said, extracting herself from the circle of his arms and reaching down to pick up the file folder she had left on the sofa. "Have you heard that there's a problem with the Garden Room banquet tonight?"

Carter shook his head.

"I thought you might have already dealt with it. Alain left a message for me this morning - something about the dinner menu being changed at the last minute. He's furious, and he's threatening to quit rather than cook what he is calling 'swine food'. You know how temperamental he is. What do you think?"

"I think this is your decision. Since you're going to be running this hotel yourself in a couple of weeks, you should decide for yourself what to do with Alain."

Carter was right. When Randolph Place opened at the end of the month, Carter was taking charge of the new hotel, and Lisa was being named manager of the Randolph Plaza. It was time she started taking charge, instead of asking Carter's opinion before she acted.

"Then I'd better go and see if I can calm him down. The last thing we need is to lose one of the city's best chefs, especially when it's convention season. I'll see you for dinner tonight."

Carter curved his finger under her chin and lifted her face to meet his. "Tonight...I could stay ..."

"No you can't," Lisa stated emphatically. "You know how I feel about waiting until we're married."

Carter groaned. "Yes, I know. You've made it perfectly clear on more than one occasion. It's a good thing this wedding is only a few weeks away."

Lisa laughed, her eyes softening. "I want our wedding night to be special, a night to remember."

"Believe me, any night I spend making love with you would be a night to remember. It's only because I love you so desperately that I'm willing to go through this torture."

Lisa reached up and threw her arms around his neck. "I know. And I love you for it." With a quick kiss, she turned and left, heading to the bank of elevators.

A short time later, Lisa emerged from the elevator on the main floor of the hotel. As she crossed the lobby on her way to the main kitchen area, her trained eyes took in the activity around her. She paused for a moment near the main entrance, acknowledging the same thrill she got every morning when she came through the revolving door into the foyer. A smile tugged at the corners of her mouth, and she knew why.

She recognized the perverse pleasure she always felt when she knew something that others didn't. In this case, it was simply that she was aware of how difficult it was to make a hotel run smoothly and efficiently without any apparent effort. Behind the seemingly calm and serene outward appearance was a staff of over three hundred, each with their own personalities and foibles. Yet here, in the grand lobby, none of it showed.

The hushed interior of the Randolph Plaza was a model of quiet elegance. Uniformed bellboys flitted unobtrusively through the lobby, hidden behind huge luggage racks. Telephones rang; computer screens flickered.

"Lisa?" A voice whispered from behind her.

Lisa turned to see the manager of Guest Services, approaching. "Hi Janice," she said with a smile. At the concerned expression on the woman's face, her smile faded. "Something wrong?"

"I'm not sure," Janice replied. "There's a man here to see you. He was here this morning while you were out. He said that he needs to speak to you urgently."

"Did he give you his name?"

Janice shook her head. "He only told me that he's an old friend."

"Where is he?"

"Over there," Janice said, pointing a finger towards the reservation desk.

The man was facing away from Lisa, and his hip rested against the desk. As if he knew he was being watched, he straightened and turned to face her.

The blood drained from her face. The floor rocked beneath her feet, and she grabbed blindly at the back of one of the stuffed armchairs dotting the lobby for support.

She stared wordlessly at the tall figure as he began to move towards her. It was like a dream, or one of those television commercials where the scenery is fuzzy and the actors are moving in slow motion. The two main characters are the only ones in focus.

And one of the characters in focus was a man who looked exactly like Jack Brennan. Not the Jack Brennan of years ago, the high-school senior who'd broken her heart, but an older version of the boy he'd once been.

There was so much about this man which was like the old Jack—the coffee-coloured hair, the wide forehead, the eyes so dark they were almost black framed by the longest lashes she had ever seen, the classically straight nose, the lips that had kissed her senseless so many times.

But there were differences, too. The man who stood before her was at least twenty pounds heavier than Jack. His light tan jacket hung open, and Lisa could tell by the body-hugging t-shirt underneath that every pound was in the right place. His hair was the same dark brown, but it grew longer now, curling slightly at the nape of his neck.

Still, there was no denying it. It was Jack.

"Lisa, are you all right?"

Janice's voice filtered through the haze in her brain. Suddenly, Lisa realized that activity at the reservation desk had stopped, and all eyes were on her. Her heart pounded, and the sandwich she'd eaten for lunch threatened to make a second appearance.

What was Jack doing here? She hadn't seen or heard from him in years, and although she would never forget him, the memories of their time together had been packed away in the recesses of her mind, much like the way a souvenir of a special occasion gradually makes its way into the back of a drawer.

Every once in a while, a sound or a particular

aroma would trigger the memories, but for the most part, she'd put those days behind her. She'd gone on and had built a life for herself. And a pretty successful one at that.

And now Jack was here. But why?

In two or three strides, Jack erased the short distance between them. He was so close that Lisa had to raise her head to meet his smile. He hadn't changed his brand of aftershave, she noticed, inhaling the fresh scent assaulting her senses. Why did that pop into her head? As if his grooming was important...

"Hi," he said softly. "Hey, I'm sorry. I knew you'd be surprised to see me, but I didn't think it would send you into a tailspin. You look like you've seen a ghost."

The room *was* spinning, and for a moment, Lisa was afraid she would actually faint. But her pride prevented it. She couldn't let him see how much his sudden appearance had affected her. He would probably enjoy seeing her swoon right in front of his nose. He'd always been pretty arrogant about the effect he had on her.

She gazed up at him, concentrating on keeping her expression blank, refusing to return his smile. That would show him, she thought. In the old days, she never could resist his smile.

"Hello, Jack," she said in a tight voice.

Jack didn't speak. He just stood there, his dark eyes roving from her hair to her feet then back again. Why didn't he say something? Anything? The silence was unbearable. "How are you?" she asked finally. Not that she cared, but politeness won out.

Pretty good," he replied. "You look great, but then you always were perfect."

Some things never change, she thought. The same old Jack. But this time she wasn't a schoolgirl with a crush on the captain of the football team. So why did that familiar warmth creep across her face just because he gave her a smile.

"I looked for you for so long and couldn't find you," he said. "I gave up. And then, this morning, out of the blue, there you were."

He couldn't have been looking very hard. She hadn't exactly gone into hiding when she left Sandpiper Key to go back to college in Virginia. Yes, her parents had sold the house and moved away a few weeks later, but it wouldn't have taken Sherlock Holmes to track her down if he'd really wanted to.

"Why were you looking for me?" she asked softly. Not that it really mattered, she told herself. He couldn't hurt her now.

Jack glanced around. He gave Janice a pointed look, and she slid quietly away from Lisa's side. Two of the bellboys were leaning against a luggage rack, watching the scene unfold. He gestured towards them, indicating that they had an audience. "Do you really think we should discuss our private life right here in the middle of a hotel lobby?"

Hot color rose instantly to her face. "We don't have a private life."

He raised an eyebrow at her and smiled. "Oh? That's not the way I remember it, but we can walk down memory lane another time. Right now, I really need to talk to you. It's important."

"There was a time when what you said was important to me. Now nothing you have to say matters. I don't want to talk to you, so if you'll excuse me, I have work to do." She turned to walk away.

"Lisa, wait a minute." Lean, tanned fingers wrapped around her hand. "Please listen to me."

At the moment of contact, a current shot through her. If she didn't know better, she'd think she'd touched a live electrical wire. No, she swore. Not now. He couldn't still have that effect on her. She wouldn't allow it.

She tugged her hand out of his but she couldn't help herself. She turned back to face him. "I listened to you once before. I don't make the same mistake twice."

"Then I'll say it quickly before you run away again. You can't get married."

A humorless laugh escaped her. "And why not?"

Jack glanced around the lobby, then leaned in close to her ear. The scent of his aftershave and his minty breath wafted over her. His voice lowered to a whisper. "Because we're still legally married. You're still my wife."

THREE

is wife? What kind of sick joke was he playing? She'd never been his wife, not in the ways that mattered. There was a time she'd believed she'd spend the rest of her life with Jack, but that had lasted all of five minutes. Not even long enough for the ink on their marriage license to dry.

A cold chill seeped through her, and her heart skipped a beat.

"We're still married," he repeated, slowly pronouncing each word. "The divorce wasn't legal."

Her eyes searched his face for a sign that this was his idea of a practical joke, but from the frown creasing his wide forehead and the pained expression in his dark eyes, she sensed that somehow, what he was telling her was true.

How could this have happened? How could they still be husband and wife after all this time? The trip they'd taken to Las Vegas the summer of her nineteenth birthday had lasted practically as long as their marriage did. Only three weeks later, he'd asked for a divorce. He'd promised he would look after everything. He'd let her go on with her life assuming that she was free. And now, after almost twelve years...

"You're lying." Please God, she prayed silently, please make this be a lie. Yet one glance at his face told her the truth.

Guilt filled his eyes. "It's hard to explain," he began. "But we're still married, at least legally. So you can't get married again or you'll be breaking the law. Bigamy."

"I can't believe you'd do this to me…"

"I didn't do this *to* you. I was as shocked as you are when I found out. Now can we please go somewhere quiet and I'll explain to you what happened?"

"I'm not going anywhere with you."

"You'd rather to be the number one topic of conversation around here?"

Lisa scanned the hotel lobby. Although most of the guests had no idea what was happening between her and Jack, several staff members were obviously trying to hear what was being said while appearing to be nonchalantly carrying out their duties. Others watched the exchange with undisguised interest, although they were too far away to hear, only to see her face that she knew was flushed and her trembling hands.

By continuing their conversation in the middle of the lobby, Lisa was only adding grist to the gossip mill. In fact, knowing how quickly rumors spread, she had no doubt that, within minutes, Carter would know about Jack's appearance. And by the time the story reached his ears, no doubt the story would have morphed into one where Lisa was carrying on a torrid affair with Jack in full view of everyone in the lobby.

In a daze, Lisa allowed Jack to lead her outside. Misty rain was falling when they exited the automatic doors and stepped out under the portico roof. Porters were unloading three limousines, and guests were wandering in and out, so the area was too crowded to have a conversation.

The fronds of the Queen Anne palms lining the driveway to the main entrance rustled as she stepped out of the protection of the portico and wrapped her arms around her waist and pulled her suit jacket closed. The sky was slate-grey, almost the same shade as the short pleated skirt she wore. The weather seemed appropriate somehow.

"Let me buy you a cup of coffee and we'll talk."

She knew she shouldn't, but her head seemed to move on its own when she found herself nodding.

Jack didn't speak as they made their way down the street until they came to a small café a few doors away from the hotel. They were both soaked by the time he ushered her inside and the air conditioning hit her. She shivered.

The café was almost empty, so Jack led her to an empty booth in the back corner where they could talk privately. He slipped into the seat beside her, so close to her that his warmth radiated from him, seeping into her chilled skin. The tangy scent of his aftershave filled her nose. His dark eyes were only inches from hers, gazing at her with...what was it? Regret?

The years faded away. A slow tingle started in her toes and wove its way through her nerve endings. Her heart thundered in her ribs, and her throat threatened to close.

No! She wouldn't allow him to resurrect all those old emotions. She wouldn't allow him to affect her. Not now. Not after all this time. Hadn't she learned anything at all in the years she'd been alone?

A twenty-something server approached the table, barely acknowledging Lisa but offering Jack a two-thousand-watt smile.

"Coffee?" Jack asked her.

She nodded.

"Do you want a menu?"

"No. Just coffee."

Jack ordered their coffee. "And a blueberry Danish," he added as the server moved away to greet another customer who'd just walked in.

Her throat tightened at the memory of how they'd often share a blueberry Danish at Lucy's Diner when they were in high school.

Lisa waited until the server was out of earshot before she spoke again. "How could you do this to me? How could you come back here and destroy my life again?"

Jack shifted to face her, then reached out and clasped her hand in both of his. She yanked it out of his grip. Her emotions were already in an uproar. She couldn't bear physical contact.

"You think I did this on purpose?"

"How could this have happened? You said you'd take care of it."

Before he had a chance to answer, the server arrived with two mugs of coffee and the Danish. "Anything else?" she asked, smiling openly at Jack. It was clear she was offering more than food.

Jack returned her smile. "No thanks."

Was the man really that blind? It sure seemed that way. Strange, she thought. The old Jack would have had a ten-minute flirt session with the server, not given her a cursory send-off.

"It's really good to see you again," he said softly after the server left. His dark eyes were only inches from hers. "And I didn't come here to destroy your life, as you put it. I came to try to save your life."

Lisa laughed bitterly. "Always so dramatic, aren't you?"

"Okay, not save your life in the literal sense, but at least maybe save you whole lot of humiliation. I figure that since my family still lives on Sandpiper, if you'd found out that we're still legally married, you would have contacted me before you went and got yourself engaged to another guy."

"Of course I would." Lisa began to tremble. What was the matter with her? It was that voice. It wasn't fair. No man should have a voice like that, so sexy and compelling.

She pulled away and reached for the mug, taking a long, slow, steadying sip. It clattered as her quaking fingers replaced it in the saucer. Coffee sloshed over the sides and puddled on the Formica table. "Well? Are you going to tell me what happened? How can we possibly still be married. You got the divorce—"

"I thought I got the divorce."

Lisa's brows furrowed in a frown. She glared at him. "If it wasn't a divorce, then what in blazes was it?" she asked, her voice little more than a harsh whisper.

"Let me explain," Jack said softly, leaning closer. "Please."

Lisa slumped back on the padded vinyl upholstery and folded her arms across her chest. Her eyes narrowed and her lips pressed into a thin line. "Let's hear it."

"My parents offered to 'take care of my lapse in judgement', as they put it, but I refused. I felt that it was something I should do myself. One of the guys at school told me I could get a quickie divorce if I went back to Vegas. I told you about that."

She remembered that day distinctly. The pain, the hurt, the tears she'd cried as she'd watched him drive away. But she wouldn't tell him that.

"So that's what I did," he went on. "You got the final divorce papers, didn't you?"

Lisa nodded, recalling the large legal-sized manilla envelope bearing the name of a law firm in Las Vegas she'd received a few weeks later. She'd signed the first batch of documents she'd received and sent them back. When the final divorce papers came, she'd read them and filed them in her bottom drawer along with the copy of their marriage certificate.

She was stunned by the wave of poignant feeling that washed over her. As if it were only yesterday, an unmistakeable sense of loss filled her, exactly like when she'd received the documents. She'd known a divorce was the right thing for both of them. She'd expected the papers, had been waiting for them. But when they'd arrived, she'd felt...empty. The envelope still held the marks of the tears she had sobbed as she'd read the words ending their marriage, each word ripping into her heart.

"So what's the problem?" Lisa prodded.

Jack poured a stream of sugar into his coffee from the glass container on the table. "The problem is this," he said, measuring his words carefully, "The lawyer who handled our divorce wasn't a lawyer at all."

Disbelief roared through her brain, coming out in a whoosh of breath. "What?"

"I hate to say it, but I got scammed."

"What?" Her brain refused to function, and she knew she was starting to sound like an idiot, but that was the only word that would come out.

So," he said, a wry grin crossing his face, "like it or not, you're still my wife."

Lisa was stunned. "And the divorce papers—"

Jack shrugged. "Aren't worth the ink it took to sign them. And we're not the only ones. Apparently he scammed more than five hundred couples—"

"How could you not know?" she asked in exasperation, her voice carrying across the diner above the racket of clattering dishes and muffled conversations. Several other diners turned to look in their direction. She lowered her voice to a whisper, but she couldn't hide the fury raging through her.

"Did you?" he countered.

"Well...no...I didn't, but—"

"Then how did you expect me to know? The papers looked legit."

Lisa shrugged and dropped her gaze, trying to make sense of what Jack was telling her. "I don't know," she said, running her hand through her hair in frustration. "I just expected you to take care of things. I trusted you."

"For Heaven's sake, Lisa," Jack said, leaning closer to her, "we were kids. I didn't screw up on purpose, you know."

Jack looked so miserable and unhappy that Lisa's anger threatened to crumble. She'd never been able to stay angry with him for long. "I know," she said with a resigned sigh. "It's just that...now...how did you find out?"

"It was a fluke. I was at a party a few weeks ago. One of the guys there is a lawyer and he was telling us about this case where a guy set up shop and scammed a lot of people before he finally got caught. He happened to mention the guy's name and it was such an unusual name that it sounded familiar. When I got home, I dragged out the papers and sure enough, it was the same guy."

Questions tumbled through Lisa's mind. "Why didn't you do what needed to be done then?"

"Because, sweetheart," he replied, "I thought I should talk to you first."

"Don't call me sweetheart!"

"Sorry," he mumbled. "Anyway, I tried to find you—

again. With the internet, I was sure you'd be on Facebook or Twitter."

"I'm not."

"I know that now. I couldn't believe you were invisible in the age of the internet. Who in the 21st century isn't on social media?"

"Lots of people," she insisted. "I use it at work. I see no reason to use it in my personal life. Anyway, that's beside the point."

He nodded. "I was about to hire a private investigator to find you, and then this morning, there you were, about to get married. The thing is, if you do get married now, you'll be a bigamist, which happens to be a criminal offense. I don't want to see you behind bars. As I recall, you never did look good in horizontal stripes. Made you look shorter than you already are. Oh, wait a minute, they wear orange jumpsuits now, right? Nope, orange isn't your color either."

Lisa recognized Jack's attempt at humor, but she was in no mood for his flippant attitude even if it was familiar to her. He'd always managed to see the humor in every situation, and always used jokes to deal with anything unpleasant. "I don't believe this," Lisa said, her chest heaving. "I'm getting married soon and you're telling me that I'm going to go to jail if I do."

"I'm sorry." His voice was tender, almost sympathetic.

"Stop saying you're sorry," she admonished. "Sorry doesn't help at this point, does it?"

"No, I guess it doesn't," he said. "But at least you

know now. So why don't you just postpone the wedding until we get this straightened out?"

Lisa's eyes widened. "Are you out of your mind? I can't do that. Carter would never—"

"You've never told him about us, have you?"

"That's none of your business," she snapped.

"I didn't think so."

It wasn't that she'd deceived Carter intentionally. She supposed that 'forgetting' to tell him was deceit. Guilt by omission, or something like that. In that case, she was definitely guilty. At the beginning of their relationship, it hadn't seemed important to bring up that blip of time in her past. Later, she'd tried to find the right time, but somehow that time never came. Then she'd reasoned that since that part of her life was over, there was no reason to drag up the painful memories again. Now it looked like she'd have no choice.

"Don't you think you should have told him you've been married before?"

"No," she blurted, "and I don't want him to find out. He...he wouldn't understand ..." Carter, think-everything-through-thoroughly Carter, would never be able to understand how the magic of the moment, and two hormonally-overcharged kids, could make common sense disappear.

Jack smiled at her then, that slow, sensual smile that used to turn her knees to water.

She looked away, her gaze focusing on the rivulets of water trickling their way down the outside of the window.

He reached over and took her hand in his. He lifted

it and examined it as the fluorescent light reflected on the ring on her finger. "That's quite a rock," he commented, running his thumb over the stone.

Warmth flowed up her arm and through her body right to the tips of her toes. She snatched her hand away and folded her arms across her chest. Suddenly, the ring seemed pretentious, garish. She tucked her hand under her other arm to hide the ring.

"We have to fix this."

"We will."

Something in the tone of his voice made her suspect he wasn't quite as adamant about finalizing this divorce as she was. "I'll take care of it myself, since I need it done by Monday."

His forehead creased in a frown. "Why? What's happening on Monday? You're not getting married then, are you?"

"We're getting our marriage license."

"You can try, but I don't think it's possible to sort out this mess by then," he said. "Law and government don't hurry anything. So I suggest you tell him before he finds out."

She slumped back against the vinyl back. How was she ever going to explain this to Carter?

FOUR

"Is there something I can do for you, Jack?"

Jack's secretary followed meekly behind him when he stormed into his office after leaving Lisa at the hotel. He stood near the windows staring out at the dismal Miami skyline, his hands clenched into fists at his sides and his features creased in a murderous scowl.

"Jack?"

Jack turned and leaned his back against the window, resting his hips on the ledge. He forced a thin smile for the young woman standing near the doorway looking as if she was ready to make a quick getaway if she needed to. "I'm sorry if I frightened you, Ruth."

She smiled back shyly. "Oh, no. I was just worried. Is anything wrong?"

"No. Nothing at all." He glanced at the Rolex on his wrist. "Look, it's almost three. Why don't you pack up and get out of here. Get an early start on the weekend."

She brightened. "Are you sure you don't need me? The documents for your meeting on Monday are on your desk, but I could stay and organize your calendar—"

"No. That's fine, but thanks for the offer. We'll take care of it next week. Now, go. Wish your boys luck for me at the baseball tournament."

"Thanks. Well, enjoy your weekend."

Jack returned to his desk and dropped into the leather chair. A stack of papers waited for his signature, and he started to proofread the correspondence, but the words just blended together, making no sense. Finally, after reading the same paragraph three times, he gave up. Every time he glanced at one of the letters in front of him, Lisa's face stared back at him.

He got up and slammed his fist on the desk. What was the matter with him? He'd been quite happy—well, at least reasonably content—with his life. He'd put the past behind him and gone on, burying himself in his work, turning his small business into a huge corporation that employed hundreds of people. It was a major accomplishment for someone so young, and he'd even had his picture on the cover of Fortune Magazine.

Now, instead of worrying about the biggest deal in the company's history, a brown-eyed pixie of a woman had taken control of his thoughts. And his hormones.

Just yesterday, he'd been toying with the idea of asking his secretary out, knowing that she was available and willing. Willing to do more than go to dinner, too, if he wasn't misjudging the signals she was sending out.

And now...

He hadn't meant to upset Lisa. He'd expected her to be surprised at his sudden appearance, and he'd gone to the hotel to try to explain to her what had happened, to try to make things right. When he'd found out that their divorce wasn't legal, he'd immediately called his attorney, who'd advised him to find Lisa, pointing out that if she'd married in the meantime, she would be guilty of a felony.

So he'd tried to locate her. He'd called old friends, the high school alumni association, and had even put an ad in the Sandpiper Key Weekly. He'd looked for her on every social media platform as well as done internet searches. Nothing.

He'd even made a call to a private investigator whose newspaper ad screamed "I can find anybody...anywhere.

But the PI hadn't had to find her, because suddenly, out of the blue, there she was. She was smiling at Jack through a TV screen, and it was as if the years had melted away, and she was smiling at him the way she had that night...

He groaned aloud as he recalled her shocked expression when she saw him standing in the hotel lobby that morning. He hadn't realized that his appearance would affect her so drastically. It had actually scared him a little when he saw her grip a chair to steady herself.

In that instant, he knew he'd never really let her go. That was why he'd never gotten married again, why he couldn't make a commitment to any other woman. The sudden revelation slammed into him.

As he'd stood beside her in the hotel lobby, he'd been seventeen again and he'd seen her for the first time. She was sitting across from him in the chemistry lab, her face half hidden as she leaned over a microscope. Her hair hung below her shoulders then, and he remembered the overwhelming urge he'd had to run it through his fingers just to see if it felt as silky as it looked.

He'd known then that this was the girl he was meant to spend his life with.

She'd glanced up and smiled shyly at him before a blush pinked her cheeks and she'd turned away.

Less than two years later, she'd smiled up at him again as they stood before a Justice of the Peace in a wedding chapel somewhere on the Las Vegas strip, promising to 'love, honor and cherish until death do us part'.

He didn't have any idea how he was going to stop her, but he knew he couldn't let her make those promises to another man.

He could go to Randolph and tell him everything. If Randolph was even remotely like his own family, the threat of any kind of scandal would be enough to outweigh emotion.

That might stop Lisa from marrying him, but at what cost?

The rest of the afternoon passed in a blur for Lisa. Somehow she managed to soothe Alain's ego, and convince him that only someone with his talents in the kitchen could transform 'swine food' into a gourmet delight.

Like an automaton, she dealt with the other minor crises that were part of her daily routine, until finally she felt as if she would explode.

There was only one way to deal with the pent-up tension, the same way she'd dealt with it since she was a little girl. Donning a pair of spandex bicycle shorts and a t-shirt, she made her way to the hotel gym on the seventh floor, a huge room filled with state-of-the art exercise equipment. Waving hello to several guests as she entered, she headed toward the back of the room where a row of empty treadmills waited. She needed to run, to hear the pounding of her heart beating in her ears, to feel the perspiration trickling down her back, to feel the muscles burn.

Luckily for her, Carter was tied up in a meeting with the bank president all afternoon to discuss the hotel's bleak financial picture. They planned to have a late supper at a small Italian restaurant near her apartment before he flew out to New York in the morning.

She couldn't face him, she realized. She couldn't bear to see the love and trust in his eyes and know how hurt he'd be when she told him the truth. No, she'd have to wait, at least until she had a chance to sort through her emotions and plan a course of action.

That decided, as soon as she got back to her office, she picked up the phone and left a message on his voicemail breaking their date. He'd be disappointed. She knew that, but she wouldn't be decent company tonight anyway. She'd explain everything when she saw him again.

He would be out of town for the rest of the week, so hopefully, by the time he returned, the whole problem would be fixed. He'd still be hurt and angry, which was to be expected, but at least she could go to him with the matter resolved, and they could put it behind them and go on with their plans.

It was almost six o'clock when she finally left the hotel. The downtown traffic was horrendous, as usual, and it took her almost an hour to drive to her condo. Finally, she turned down a side street and pulled into the underground garage.

Struggling with her briefcase and a bag of groceries, she carefully made her way to the elevator and took it to her apartment.

Inside, she kicked off her shoes and padded through to her bedroom, dropping her purse and the grocery bag on the kitchen counter as she passed.

The divorce papers were exactly where she'd left them, tucked in the bottom drawer of her bedside table, beneath the corsage from her high school prom and the photographs at the beach...

She remembered that day, the scorching sun, the sparkling water, the warmth of the sand on her back, the heat of Jack's kisses after the sun had disappeared ...

Lisa shook herself from her traitorous memories and slammed the drawer shut. Automatically, she stripped off her clothes and pulled on a turquoise terrycloth bathrobe.

Then she filled the tub with hot water and her favourite bath salts. As she relaxed in the steamy water, the memories came unbidden into her mind, and tears filled her eyes. She didn't want to remember that summer. It was still too painful...

"Let's get married!"

Lisa's eyes flew open. She couldn't have heard right. The champagne was making her hallucinate. "What?"

Jack gripped both her arms and she gazed up at him. "I mean it, Lisa. Let's get married."

"You're drunk, Jack."

"I've only had one glass of champagne. Now what do you say? Will you marry me?"

"Get out of here. You're crazy."

Jack kissed her hard. "I'm crazy about you. And I'll go crazy if you don't marry me and say you'll be mine forever."

"You can't be serious."

"I've never been more serious in my life. I love you. You love me. It's simple."

"Don't be ridiculous. It isn't simple at all. We can't get married."

"Why not?"

"Because we don't have a license, that's why."

"Then we'll get one."

"We still can't get married."

"Why not?"

"Because...because..."

"Don't you love me?"

"Of course I do. Don't be silly. But getting married..."

"Lisa, I'm going back to school the day after we get home, and you're leaving next day. We won't be able to see each other again until Thanksgiving. I can't stand the thought that you'll meet someone else..."

"I won't."

"If we're married, then I'll know you're mine."

"But so soon? What about our parents. They'll be furious."

"They can't do anything about it. Lisa, please marry me. Today."

Why did the thought of being Jack's wife seem so right? All the logical reasons why not flitted through her mind. They were too young, too inexperienced in life, too...much in love.

Jack was worried she might find someone else when she went away to school, but what about him? Maybe he would find another girl. Fear of losing Jack snaked through her.

"Okay."

An hour later, they were back in their hotel room, a marriage license in Jack's wallet. With a grin, Jack pulled out a local telephone book and found a chapel within a block of the hotel. "I'll be back in a flash," he promised as he bounded off the bed and disappeared out the door. True to his word, and reappeared a half hour later with their two friends, Carol and Phil.

When Lisa asked where he'd been, he grinned, "You'll see." And he wouldn't say any more.

They held hands as they walked down the neon-bright

street a few hours later to the wedding chapel. Lisa's legs were so unsteady she felt like she was walking through the fun house ride at the county fair. The street seemed to be moving, heaving. She giggled when she mentioned it to Jack. "You've had too much to drink," he told her. "You're not used to it."

Then they both laughed, knowing that she had only had a half glass of champagne. But she felt giddy. But maybe she was giddy at the thought of becoming Jack's wife and it had nothing to do with alcohol at all.

Two neon wedding bells blinked on and off at the entrance to the chapel. The heady perfume of roses hung in the air as Lisa and Jack opened the double doors and went inside, while Carol and Phil followed quietly behind.

Their feet sank into royal blue plush carpeting in the small foyer. An elderly woman greeted them and ushered them into a room on the right, where white satin bows adorned pews on each side of a short aisle leading to an altar. Soft music filled the room. Jack patted his jacket pocket where he had slipped their marriage license. He squeezed Lisa's hand tightly. "I love you," he mouthed as they walked towards the justice of the peace impatiently waiting for them on a raised platform at the altar.

The wedding ceremony itself was short, the words meaningless to the J.P. In fact, the man seemed bored by the whole thing. But to Lisa, it was magical. Tears of joy filled her eyes as she gazed solemnly at Jack and vowed to love, honor and cherish him forever. And she meant every word.

When the J.P. asked for the ring, Jack reached into his pocket and produced a gold wedding band engraved with tiny doves. Lisa gasped.

"I found it in a small shop near the hotel," he whispered as he placed it on her finger.

A few minutes and a few words later, they were husband and wife.

Lisa couldn't decide whether to laugh or cry. She always cried at weddings, and her eyes burned from unshed tears. It seemed inappropriate somehow to cry at your own wedding, especially if you were happy. And she was past happy. She was delirious.

"You may kiss your bride," the J.P. said, and for the first time, Lisa noticed a flicker of emotion on the man's face.

She gazed up at Jack, her heart swelling with love as his arms reached around her and drew her close. He kissed her gently, then pulled away and handed her their marriage license. "Here you are, Mrs. Brennan." Then he grabbed her and spun her around, and they laughed until they both cried. Carol hugged her. Phil pumped Jack's hand furiously. They all cried.

Mrs. Brennan. Mrs. Jack Brennan. Lisa Brennan.

Lisa smiled to herself. The words had a nice ring to them.

She practically floated down the street back toward the hotel. Carol and Phil strolled behind them, still shaking their heads in amazement at what Lisa and Jack had done.

"I think that under the circumstances, we should change our sleeping arrangements," Jack said to Phil. "Can you bunk in Carol's room tonight?"

Carol's cheeks flushed scarlet, but Lisa noticed that she didn't refuse. In fact, Carol seemed quite pleased with the change in accommodations.

Lisa's face burned. Of course. The wedding night. What had she done? For Heaven's sake, she was only nineteen *years old. She hadn't even finished college yet, and here she was a married woman. And now Jack was making plans to...Oh no!*

Lisa was trembling so violently by the time they reached the hotel that she could barely manage to walk down the corridor to his—their—room.

The 'do not disturb' sign lay on the dresser, and Jack picked it up and grinned at her before opening the door and hooking it on the handle. Lisa's face flamed.

Jack smiled at her and slipped his jacket off, draping it over a chair. "Want some more champagne?"

Lisa shook her head. Champagne was the last thing she needed. Her legs were already threatening to buckle under her, and she didn't want to think about what was happening in her stomach.

She stood in the center of the room, feeling like a fly caught in a spider's web. She was trapped. And she hadn't merely fallen into the trap, shed jumped in voluntarily.

She knew about the 'first time' and what was expected of her. But she had no idea how to go about it. There had been times during the past few months that their love-making could have gone too far, but they'd stopped in time. She'd been determined to stay a virgin until she was married.

And now, here she was. Married and clueless.

She didn't know how to please Jack, and before morning, he would already regret marrying her. He'd probably slept with lots of girls, girls who knew what he wanted and needed. He'd never told her he'd been with other girls, but he was so popular that she couldn't imagine him being as inexperienced as she was. Oh, darn, why hadn't she paid more attention when Carol had gone into detail about the intimate details of her relationship with Phil? At least then she'd know what not to do.

She held her breath and watched as Jack crossed the room and slipped her purse from her shoulder. It fell silently on the carpet. "Nervous?" he whispered in her ear.

Lisa nodded. Her voice caught in her throat. She didn't trust herself to even try to speak. She wanted to laugh and cry at the same time.

"Come here," Jack said softly, holding his arms out. She wanted to run, but instead she moved forward, right into the circle of his arms. As his arms closed around her, the uncertainty and terror she'd been feeling disappeared. This was where she wanted to be, this was where she was meant to be. She could sense that he was nervous too, and she relaxed slightly.

Jack's arms tightened around her. She lifted her face, tilting it towards him.

Jack looked down at her for a long, sweet moment. Her heart thundered in her chest, every nerve ending tingling with anticipation. Then he lowered his head and his mouth found hers, tentatively at first and then more surely as her lips opened beneath his.

For a brief moment, she thought of pulling away, telling him that she wasn't ready yet. But she was ready. She wanted his kiss, his arms around her. She needed them more than she'd ever needed anything in her life.

With passion flooding her body, Lisa tightened her arms around his neck. One hand curved into the crisp texture of his hair, the other clung to the hard muscles of his shoulders. She felt herself responding, arching closer, molding herself to the hard contours of his body. She kissed him as fervently as he kissed her, and deep, deep inside she began to melt, to let go. The feeling was exhilarating, frightening, exciting all at the same time. She gave herself to it as she gave herself to him. There was no turning back.

The shrill ringing of the telephone filtered through Lisa's brain, bringing her back to the present. She shivered in the sudsy water, now cold, and bounded out of the bathtub. Water splashed on the ceramic tiles, puddling at her feet as she wrapped a fluffy blue bath towel around herself and ran down the hall to where she'd left her cell phone on the coffee table. The caller had hung up.

Her head still pounding, she shuffled back into the bathroom, towelled herself dry before putting on a t-shirt with the Walt Disney World castle on the front and a pair of cotton pajama pants. She climbed into bed, turned on the television and switched the bedside lamp off. Perhaps if she could sleep, she could keep the memories at bay.

FIVE

heavy knock at the apartment door woke Lisa with a start. She glanced at the alarm clock on the bedside table and groaned. Six thirty-seven.

For Pete's sake, she muttered to herself as she rolled over and buried her head under her down pillow. Who in their right mind is up at this time of the morning on a Saturday?

The hammering persisted, and even the soft down of the pillow couldn't drown it out. Her visitor apparently wasn't going to go away.

"Lisa! Aren't you up yet?"

Jack. It was Jack doing his best to break down her door in the middle of the night. She *could* stay in bed, she supposed. Eventually he'd give up. Or would he? Knowing Jack's infinite stubbornness, assuming he hadn't grown out of it, he would stand out there until she eventually opened the door. But meanwhile, he would have managed to wake every tenant in the building. There was no way to avoid him.

A curse slipped past her lips as she dragged herself out of bed and shuffled to the front door. When she opened it, he was leaning on the wall directly across from her door, his hair dishevelled, a day's growth of stubble shadowing his chin. He straightened when he saw her in the doorway.

"Morning," he said brightly.

"Do you have any idea what time it is?" she hissed.

"Sure." A crooked smile crossed his face, revealing the dimples she had so often teased him about. "Six thirty or so. Why? Don't your clocks work?"

Lisa ignored his attempt at humor. "It's Saturday."

"I know that," he said.

"What are you doing here at this ungodly hour?"

"I'm trying to apologize for yesterday. I even brought a peace offering." He held up a brown paper bag and waved it in front of her nose. She recognized the logo of the bakery at the corner. "Chocolate dough-nuts. Your favorite. Can I come in?"

"Would it make any difference if I said no?"

"Of course not," he replied.

As much as he deserved it, she couldn't just slam the door in his face. She shrugged and stepped back with a nonchalance she hardly felt. "Come on in."

Jack slipped past her, filling her lungs with his spicy masculine scent, filling the room with his presence.

He paused in the middle of the living room and glanced around, then nodded his head in approval. The apartment was an open concept floor plan that

Lisa loved. Windows lined one wall, and the morning sun, only now peeking above the horizon, cast a golden glow on the combination living/dining room and the kitchen. The other room was her bedroom, leading off the small foyer. Lisa had taken months to decorate her small condo just the way she wanted it, and she had created an elegant, yet cozy atmosphere. Laura Ashley print fabrics, pastel colours, and light wood.

"Nice," he said softly. "Really nice. Somehow I always pictured you in a place like this."

Once, long ago, she'd pictured herself like this too, only she'd be waking up in the morning with Jack beside her in a cozy split-level where they'd be raising their kids. But he'd snatched that away from her without even having the courage to face her in person.

Anger rose up in her. This man had used her and thrown her away like yesterday's newspaper, she reminded herself grimly. She squared her shoulders to bolster her courage and raised her head to meet his dark eyes. "What are you doing here? I told you yesterday when I left that I'd take care of the divorce myself. At least that way I'll know it's done right."

"Ouch!"

"You deserve it," Lisa said. "I told you you don't have to worry about it. So what do you want?"

"I came to ask you to wait to go to your lawyer. I...I want...I mean I want a chance to—"

Lisa laughed bitterly. "What? Have you lost your mind?"

"Listen to me, Lisa, please," Jack began, closing the

gap between them and grasping her hands in his. "I made a mistake."

Lisa's rage was almost all-consuming. "You bet your life you made a mistake. You used me and then went on to greener pastures once you got back to school. Even at the time, I couldn't quite understand why you went out with me in the first place, the hot-shot football hero and the skinny tomboy. All the time we dated, I waited for you to leave me for someone who was prettier. And then when you asked me to marry you, I couldn't believe you wanted me—forever. But that was the only way to get me into your bed, wasn't it? And it worked."

Lisa saw the pain playing on Jack's face, and she couldn't help herself. Revenge was sweet after all. She hated herself for it, but she enjoyed seeing him flinch at her words, as if she was physically attacking him. "You took everything I had to offer, my love, my trust—and my virginity. I was so naive, so trusting. I really believed all your lies. I was so happy, I even started looking at apartments and furniture on weekends, dreaming about how it would be when we were finished school and we could be together and start a family. And then I had a visit from your mother."

"It wasn't like that—"

"Wasn't it? Then tell me, Jack, how was it?"

Jack stared into Lisa's eyes, puffy and swollen, for a few moments, saying nothing. Without a pound of concealer, she knew it was impossible to hide the dark circles under her eyes, and it was obvious that she hadn't slept much the night before. He'd know she'd spent a sleepless night because of him. That alone made her even angrier.

"I smell coffee," he said. "Could you spare a cup and I'll try to explain. Then I'll leave. I promise."

The appeal in his voice wasn't lost on Lisa. She hated it when he did that. Hadn't she learned anything at all in the years she'd been alone? Why couldn't she say no to him?

"Fine." Lisa shrugged, resigned to spending the next few minutes listening to his feeble excuses and apologies. She knew him well enough to know he wouldn't leave until she'd listened to him, so the sooner she let him finish, the sooner she could get rid of him once and for all.

Jack followed her into the small kitchen. She poured two cups of coffee and clattered them on the glass-topped table in the dining area. "So talk."

The words were changed, but he wasn't telling her anything she didn't already know—that his family had threatened to disown him, how they would have withdrawn their financial support, how he would have been forced to quit school, to give up everything he'd known, everything he'd planned for his life.

But the fact remained, he should have chosen her, not them. He should have refused. And he didn't.

"I was wrong. I shouldn't have listened to my parents. I went along with them because I always figured that once I was finished school, we could—"

"So the money came first," Lisa accused.

"Come on, Lisa! I was thinking of our future. What kind of life could I have offered you if I didn't finish school? You'd rather I had a career slinging burgers or working the night shift at the local 7-11?"

"You should have trusted me, talked to me..."

"We were nineteen years old. We were babies. I..I was wrong...I wrote to you to tell you...the letters came back unopened...I came back that Christmas—"

"What do you mean you wrote to me? What letters?"

"I wrote six times before I gave up—"

He had to be lying. He hadn't even had the decency to tell her himself that he wanted out of their marriage. She'd had to hear it from his mother. And from the time his mother showed up on her doorstep to let her know that Jack had filed for divorce, she'd never heard a word from him. "Don't lie to me, Jack. There were no letters."

Jack gazed at her, long and hard. "I had a feeling you wouldn't believe me so I brought proof." He got up and reached into his jacket pocket, pulling out a pile of envelopes secured by a rubber band. "Here," he said, offering them to her.

Her fingers were trembling as she took the envelopes and looked at her name scrawled across the front. Her mouth went dry, and she swallowed, slowly sliding the elastic band off the pile and shuffling the envelopes. They were identical, except for the postmarked dates in the top right-hand corner covering the stamp. The dates were two weeks apart, and all were dated that fall eleven years ago. And all of the envelopes had the same words written on them—" return to sender"—in handwriting that Lisa recognized as belonging to the one person she trusted most. Her mother. She felt her face pale, and the envelopes fell from her hand.

"They were returned, unopened. I thought—"

"I never saw them," she whispered hoarsely. "Honestly, I didn't—"

"Who—"

"My mother." Why? Why would her mother have done this? Lisa didn't know the answer, and she never would. Her mother had taken the answers with her to her grave when she died the year before. For some reason, her mother had intercepted Jack's letters, the letters that could have changed her life.

Jack nodded imperceptibly. "I'm not surprised," he murmured. "She didn't like me very much."

"No, she didn't. But I didn't think she hated you enough to do this." Lisa's gaze floated down to the envelopes in her hand, then back to Jack.

Jack sipped at his coffee. "When I came home for Christmas vacation, your family had moved...I didn't know where to find you..."

Lisa felt her anger towards him slipping away. "We moved right after that. My mother told us that she'd received an inheritance, and we had to leave immediately. Well," she went on, "it doesn't matter now. That's all water under the bridge, as they say."

"You're wrong. It does matter. I should've come back instead of writing those letters. You've spent all these years thinking I didn't want you..."

Lisa got up and turned away from him.

So you forgive me?" Jack asked.

Forgive wasn't the word Lisa would have chosen. Accepted, maybe. Resigned, perhaps. In the years since she'd last seen Jack, Lisa had gone on with her life, a little harder, a little less trusting.

"Sure," she said softly, hoping her even voice disguised the turmoil going on inside her. If it would make Jack feel better, she'd ease his conscience. "It was a long time ago, and time has a way of healing old hurts."

"Are you?"

"Am I what?"

"Are you healed?" he asked softly. "Really healed?"

Lisa's voice caught in her throat. No, she thought, she would never heal completely. There would always be scars. "Of course," she lied. "I'm happy now. I have a satisfying career, and I'm going to marry the man I love."

"You don't really love him."

Lisa nodded. "Of course I do. Very much."

"The way we loved each other?"

"Absolutely," she answered a little too quickly.

What could she say? No, she didn't love Carter the way she'd loved Jack. She would never give herself completely to another man, would never feel that their souls were intertwined the way she had when she and Jack had been together. But she did love him.

Her love for Carter was different, more mature, but just as real. They were a perfect match. Everyone said so. They both enjoyed the same things, quiet dinners, theatre, travel. They were both career-oriented, and they'd both been hurt in the past. Their relationship was based on mutual respect and affection, and neither one expected more than the other had to give.

"But do you have fun with him? Do you do goofy things like we used to do?"

Lisa was incensed. "Only children should do silly things. And of course I have fun. Not that it's any of your business. Why would you ask a question like that?"

"Because we always laughed so much. That was the first thing I noticed about you. Your laugh. It made me think of sunshine and summer…and soda fizz."

"Soda fizz?"

"Uh-huh. Bubbly. Silly, I guess, but that's how I felt."

Lisa smiled softly, remembering the laughter they'd shared...

"The last thing you need is a man who doesn't give you laughter. You need that...do you remember when we went horseback riding with the gang at Mussel-man's Lake?" he asked, as he sipped his coffee.

Lisa did remember. The memory of that summer day brought an unbidden shadow of a smile to her face. "You could have found me a horse that was a little more placid."

"I thought you knew how to handle animals."

"Only one two-legged one," she retorted.

"That's true. You were an expert at handling me when I got out of control."

Lisa couldn't let that comment pass. "And you were usually more of a beast than any horse, even one called Cyclone."

Jack chuckled, the sound of his laughter deep and

rich. "It didn't occur to any of us that you could've been seriously hurt on that horse. But you must admit it was funny seeing you hanging onto that horse's mane, screaming at the top of your lungs. You had the poor horse so terrified he kept running faster just to try to get away from you."

Lisa couldn't help it, and within moments, they were both giggling like children. She remembered that later, when the six of them were wolfing down cheeseburgers and Cokes at a local restaurant, she had seen the funny side of the matter, too, and had laughed with the rest of them.

"Don't tell me you didn't have fun that day," he said, smiling. "And later, we had a good time, didn't we? That is, until you made me take you home."

Lisa blushed. The evening had ended as most of their evenings did, with them parked in Jack's convertible at the beach, and Lisa calling a halt to his kisses before she lost control of her own emotions.

"Lisa," he said softly, leaning across the small kitchen table, "I made a huge mistake. And I want to make it up to you. Carter Randolph isn't the man for you. I am. All I'm asking for is a chance. Just a chance."

"You're insane, Jack. We're not kids any more. I've changed. And so have you. We can't go back to the way it was, even if I wanted to. Which I don't," she added vehemently. "I love Carter."

There went those dimples again. "You think you do, but you won't admit that you're settling for security. And you're wrong about me trying to go back. I don't want to go back to the way it was. I want to go forward, and I want it better than it was. And as soon as you stop fighting me and let me prove to you that we should be together, you'll see I'm right."

Lisa shook her head. "Go away, Jack," she said quietly. "Let me get a quiet divorce and go ahead with my life. Please."

"I can't, Lisa. It's funny, you know. I knew there was something missing in my life, but I didn't realize what it was until I saw your face smiling back at me yesterday morning on TV. It was like a sledgehammer smacking me in the head, and I knew that you were what was missing. That's why I've never been able to make a commitment to a woman all these years." He grinned sheepishly. "Not that I've been a monk, exactly. But I couldn't settle into a serious relationship. And yesterday, I finally realized why."

Lisa's mouth felt dry, and her blood started to pound through her veins. Why hadn't he told her these things eleven years ago when she had sobbed herself to sleep every night?

She sipped her coffee, keeping her eyes averted from Jack's. What could she say?

"Lisa?"

She raised her head and met his gaze. The pain in his eyes was unmistakeable. "I know you're going to file for divorce, but I'm going to fight it. I'm well aware that under the circumstances no judge in his right mind will refuse you. I don't stand a chance in court, and in time, you will get your divorce, but at least I can stall your marriage long enough that maybe you'll see that he isn't right for you."

"You don't even know Carter. How can you know whether he is right for me or not?"

Without hesitation, Jack spoke earnestly. "Because I know his kind. I deal with men like him every day. And because I'm the only man who's right for you. And one day you'll see that. I just want to make sure you aren't married to Randolph when you do."

"How can you sit there and presume to tell me who is right for me. You don't even know me anymore."

"I know you better—and I'd bet more intimately—than Carter Randolph ever will."

Lisa's cheeks flamed at the suggestive tone of his voice. She lowered her eyes, concentrating on the black liquid in the mug. She curved her hands around the cup, the heat from the coffee burning into her palms. "I ..."

Suddenly, the telephone rang. Lisa started, jarring the cup. Coffee splashed over the sides on to her hands. What was going on? Every since Jack showed up, she'd been jumpier than a Mexican jumping bean. She bounded and darted across the living room, as much to escape Jack's penetrating gaze as to answer her phone.

Carter's voice crackled through the phone. She recognized the distinct sounds of a traffic. "Did I wake you?" he asked.

"No," Lisa answered guiltily. *I'm in my pajamas, relaxing and having a cup of coffee with my husband..* She almost laughed, the situation was so bizarre. Almost like a badly written sitcom episode.

"I do apologize for calling at such an early hour, but I missed seeing you last night. I'm on my way to the airport and I'd like to stop by for a few minutes before I leave for New York. Do you mind?"

"I...I'm not dressed..."

The line crackled, cutting off conversation. "I'm sure...beautiful, no matter...wearing."

"Well..."

"...turning onto your street now..."

The line went dead. A couple of minutes. He would find Jack sitting comfortably at her kitchen table nibbling on chocolate doughnuts and drinking coffee.

How could she explain this to Carter? And would he believe her? She knew exactly what Carter would think, that Jack had been there all night. And judging by her dishevelled appearance, and Jack's beard-stubbled face, it did look that way. Circumstantial evidence, maybe. But evidence, definitely. If the situation were reversed and she arrived at Carter's apartment and found a strange woman with him at the crack of dawn, would she believe it was innocent? She doubted it.

No, she had to get rid of Jack. And soon.

"Jack," she said breathlessly as she sped back into the kitchen, "you have to get out of here. Carter's on his way over, and he can't find you here. He'll think we spent the night together."

She spun around, grabbed Jack's coat and threw it at him. "You have to go. Now. He'll be here any minute."

Jack grinned lazily and lifted his mug to his lips. "Good. I'd like to say hello."

Lisa glared at him. "You aren't going to say hello. Not now. Not ever, if I have anything to say about it."

"Why not? Doesn't he trust you?"

"That's not the point."

"It isn't?" Jacks eyebrows arched. "I think that it's a valid point. After all, if you can't trust the woman you're going to marry—"

"I don't have time to argue with you. Just get out of here."

He sighed dramatically, but got up and put on his jacket. "I'll go, but only on one condition."

Condition? She had no time for Jack and his silly games.

"Please, Jack. Not now." She was willing to plead with him just to get him out of her apartment before Carter showed up.

"Okay, but we're not done."

She was running out of time. "Fine. Just go."

He smiled, turned and made his way to the door. He had his hand on the handle when suddenly, there was a knock.

It was too late.

SIX

L isa froze, staring at the closed door. Her gaze flew to Jack, whose face was split into a wide grin. "This could be fun," he mused.

Lisa's cheeks flamed. What was she going to do? Carter knocked again, the sound like a death knell. "Just a minute, Carter," she squeaked. "I'll be right there."

She spun around and faced Jack, hoping to appeal to his sense of fairness. "Please don't do this, Jack," she began, as she grabbed his arm and began to drag him toward the open bedroom door.

She should have known that would never work. Jack's eyes lit up. "Really, Lisa," he joked, the dimples in his cheeks and mischievous twinkle infuriating her, "I don't think this is the time but if you insist—"

"Stop it! Just stay in there until I get rid of him. Please?"

"What's it worth to you?"

Even in the compromising position she had found herself in, that phrase brought a soft smile to her lips. How many times had Jack—and she—asked that same question? It had been a game of sorts that they'd played when they were teens. Everything demanded payment, and the cost was always paid happily and in full. "Not now!"

Lisa slammed the bedroom door, leaving Jack testing the comfort of her king-size bed. Her pulse raced as she hurried across the living room and let Carter in. "I'm so sorry. I didn't mean to keep you standing in the hallway."

Carter leaned over and brushed a kiss on her cheek. "I must admit I was beginning to wonder what was taking so long."

She forced a laugh. "Oh, you know, girl stuff."

Over Carter's shoulder, she noticed a movement at the bedroom door. Jack had opened it a crack and was watching her, listening to every word. A smile creased his face, and he winked at her.

"Your face is flushed, darling. Do you still have your headache?" Carter's tone was sympathetic.

"I ..." Here was a golden opportunity, one she couldn't afford to miss. "Yes...I do."

"You look exhausted. Is that why you were already up when I called?"

"I...yes...I was getting a painkiller."

Carter slid his arms around Lisa's waist, pulling her closer to him. She hoped that he couldn't hear the pounding of her heart. "Would you like me to stay for a few minutes? My plane doesn't leave for a couple of hours. I could make you tea, or massage your temples."

"No," she blurted out, "I...I just want to go back to bed..."

In her peripheral vision, she noticed Jack nod his head in agreement. A grin split his face. She glared at him. Turning her attention back to Carter, she gave him a weak smile. "I apologize for breaking our dinner date last night, but I had such a headache, all I wanted to do was sleep."

"Don't worry about it, darling. We'll make up for it when I get back. In fact, we'll be having dinner together on Saturday night."

Lisa frowned. Saturday? She couldn't think, not with Jack eyeing her from the bedroom door.

"Did you forget?" Carter asked. "Mother's benefit dinner."

"No," she assured him. "How could I forget that?" The dinner at Randolph Central. With everything that had happened since yesterday, she'd completely forgotten about the benefit dinner Carter's mother was hosting for Children in Crisis, the charity she was heavily involved with.

"I'm sure I'll be fine by then," she told him. "What time are we expected?"

"Cocktails are at seven. Dinner at eight. My flight gets in at five, so I'll pick you up just after six. That gives us plenty of time to mingle before dinner. What do you think?"

"That'll be fine, Carter. I'll be ready."

"Oh," Carter said, as if a thought had suddenly occurred to him. "I hear you had a visitor yesterday."

Lisa's heart began to thump so hard she was sure Carter could hear it.

"Uh...yes, I did...an old friend."

"Oh?" Carter's eyebrows raised in question.

"Yes...just someone I knew when I lived on Sandpiper Key. He was just passing through..."

"I heard you seemed very upset. And then when you called to cancel our dinner engagement—"

"Oh, you know how rumors are. I wasn't upset, just surprised. And I *did* have that terrible headache."

Carter seemed satisfied with her explanation, and Lisa took a deep steadying breath.

"I see," he said. "I became a little concerned when I got your message, that's all."

"I'm fine. Honestly." *And I'm getting really good at lying.*

Carter's lips closed in on hers, and Lisa tried to forget that Jack was peeking through the door. Jack wants a show, she thought vindictively, I'll give him a show. She leaned into Carter's kiss, winding her arms around his neck and pressing her body against his.

"I've heard of women who say 'not tonight, I have a headache'. But if this is how headaches affect you, I'm all for it," Carter breathed huskily as they separated and she gently guided him towards the front door.

Lisa smiled grimly. "I have a feeling I'll be having a lot of headaches for the next little while," she murmured, knowing that Jack would perceive the double meaning in her words.

Carter cupped her chin in his hand and ran his thumb over her cheek. "I love you," he whispered, dropping a kiss on her forehead. Then he turned and started walking down the corridor to the elevators.

"Have a good flight," Lisa called after him. "I'll miss you."

"Not nearly as much as I'll miss you," Carter vowed as the light above the elevator blinked and the doors slid open. He waved, then disappeared inside.

Almost before she'd had a chance to close the door, Jack appeared at her side. "How could you watch us like that?" she said, her voice almost a hiss.

"I just wanted to see true love in action," he said innocently. "A little forced, wasn't it?"

So she hadn't fooled him after all.

"You are impossible," she said, crossing the living room to the kitchen. "Why don't you go away and leave me alone?"

Jack gazed upward, seeming to consider her request for a minute, then grinned. "What's it worth to you?"

Lisa groaned. She didn't want to play this game. There was no answer she could give that wouldn't create problems for her. So instead, she replied, "What is it going to cost me?"

Jack leaned against the kitchen counter and crossed his arms in front of him, gazing at Lisa with undisguised desire.

Even after all these years, she recognized the look in his dark eyes. "No way."

"What did I say? I'm insulted."

No, she hadn't mistaken the look, but she decided to let it go. "What do you want, Jack?"

"A kiss."

"What?"

"One kiss. One kiss like the one you gave Carter. Then I'll leave."

"That's blackmail."

Jack grinned. "I prefer to think of it as an incentive."

The silence in the room was broken only by the ticking of the grandfather clock in the hall. Jack and Lisa stared at each other, Jack waiting for her answer, Lisa trying to find a way out.

Kissing Jack Brennan would be the worst thing she could possibly do. After all, she was engaged to another man. Allowing Jack to kiss her would be almost like being unfaithful to Carter. Besides, she had an unwelcome premonition of what the touch of Jack's lips would do to her. She couldn't risk it.

"What's the matter, Lisa? Are you afraid that you might still feel something for me?"

"You really have a high opinion of yourself, don't you? Well, I have news for you. I'm not the timid seventeen-year-old anymore who went ga-ga over the big muscular football player. You think I'm going to fall into your arms, and forget everything? Well, it isn't going to happen. My feelings for you died a long time ago."

She voiced the words as if she truly believed them, but Jack had given voice to the fears she had just admitted to herself. Jack's kisses had always had an effect on her, and she didn't want to find out that she was still susceptible.

Her breath fluttered, and her gaze slipped to the sensuous lines of his mouth as he moved toward her. She wanted to move away, knew that she should move away. Instead, she found herself rooted to the floor. His hands were gentle as they cupped her face, tilting it up, and even as she opened her mouth to protest, the words died in her throat. She felt his fingers thread through her hair, and although common sense told her to break free now, she stood, transfixed by his touch.

"I ..." she whispered, but her words were lost as his mouth descended to hers. When he drew her against the hard length of him, her lips were already parted, ready to join his, and a wild thick warmth rushed through her. She tried to resist, but it was impossible. She told herself that she didn't want his kiss, but an inner voice mocked her.

Fire coursed through her, sweeping away all her defences. Her hands moved upward over his shoulders, her fingers entwined around his neck. His muscles tightened under her touch, and he gave a low groan. Involuntarily, she arched against his muscled chest, and she could feel his desire.

His arms tightened around her waist, a hard, firm hold. Exploring her mouth with deliberation, he deepened the kiss until finally, he released her

She gazed up at him.

"It's still there, isn't it, Lisa?" Jack asked softly. "You can fight it from now until doomsday, but it's still there."

"No." It was a breathless protest as the beat of her heart drowned out all warnings. She shuddered, as if the frigid January wind had made its way into the warm kitchen. She backed away to the protection of one of the high-backed dining room chairs. Her fingers gripped its back with white-knuckled intensity. "You can't tell me that Carter's kisses make you feel like this ..." he breathed as he reached towards her.

"You promised to leave. Now please go," she muttered, turning away and staring sightlessly to the grey dawn outside.

"Oh, Lisa ..."

"Get out, Jack!"

As the tears began to well up, she bit her lip and held herself tense until she heard the sound of the apartment door closing. She let her body go limp and she began to cry, quietly at first, then growing until deep sobs racked her body. Whether it was for the lost dreams of youth, or for the problems of today, she didn't know. But for what seemed like an eternity, she stood at the window, her tears rolling unchecked down her cheeks.

What was she going to do?

For the third time that day, Jack repeated his message to Lisa's voicemail. Even the sound of her voice warmed him. "Lisa, it's Jack again. How many times are you going to make me apologize before you call me back. I'm sorry. I acted like a jerk. What else can I say? Please call me."

She was avoiding him. And he couldn't really blame her. He'd gone to her apartment to try to begin to make amends for what he'd done eleven years ago. He hadn't expected her to throw herself into his arms, and all he'd really hoped for was another chance. But he'd screwed it up, just like he seemed to screw up every time he went near her. Instead of taking it slow, he'd charged full speed ahead. Asking for a kiss had been one of the stupidest things he'd ever done, but he hadn't been able to resist...

"Ruth?"

Almost before the word had left his mouth, his secretary appeared in his office doorway. "Can you get me Eleanor Randolph on the phone." A smile pulled at his lips. "I'm going fishing."

Ruth didn't move. "Who's Eleanor Randolph," she asked, "and what are you fishing for?"

"Randolph Hotel group," he replied. Then, he grinned wryly and added, "Please?"

"Yes, sir," Ruth replied, then disappeared into the outer office.

People like the Randolphs irritated Jack. They reminded him of his parents and their friends, the cremé de la cremé, the upper crust of society. In their social circles, money could buy just about anything or anybody. He'd proven that himself. His parents had even bought him.

How could Lisa think she was in love with a man

like Carter Randolph? A man whose every move was calculated for effect. The intercom buzzed.

"Yes?"

"Mrs. Randolph on line one."

"Thanks," Jack muttered as he picked up the receiver and pressed the flashing button on the phone.

"Mrs. Randolph," he said, "Jack Brennan, Brennan International. How are you?"

"Mr. Brennan," she exclaimed. "It's so nice to hear from you. And I'm just fine, thank you. How are you?"

"Terrific."

"Is there something I can do for you, Mr. Brennan?" Mrs. Randolph asked. Jack noticed the hesitation in her voice, and he understood why Eleanor Randolph was wary. They'd crossed swords often in the past, usually when both of them wanted the same thing. Strange, he thought. Now it's her son and I that both want the same thing.

Jack understood Eleanor Randolph. Flattery was her Achilles heel, and he planned to use it to his advantage.

Time to throw her some bait. "I understand you're very involved with Children in Crisis."

"That's right," Mrs. Randolph answered. "It's a wonderful organization, dedicated to helping those poor unfortunate children..."

Those poor unfortunate children... Eleanor Randolph was one of society's Good Samaritans, who used their money and power to work for the many charitable organizations scrounging for funds. If her motivation was pure, he would have been impressed. But women like Eleanor Randolph had only one reason for their philanthropy—clout. He knew this because his mother was exactly the same. She used her money to try to buy her way into Heaven, playing the role of the humanitarian, while at the same time making sure that any contributions she made to her 'worthwhile causes' were tax-deductible.

Now, reel her in. "I don't have to tell you that it's well known that your unending energy and devotion is unmatched..."

"Why, Mr. Brennan, you're embarrassing me," she flustered.

This is easier than I thought it would be.

"But it's so kind of you to say…"

"I've also heard you'll be hosting a benefit dinner next Saturday night to fund a new shelter for families who are victims of abuse."

"Why, yes, that's true," she beamed. "It should be a roaring success. We've had such support—"

"I'm sure it's been a tremendous amount of work. But I don't doubt that you'll surpass your goal. Actually, that's why I'm calling," Jack interrupted. "I'd like to buy a ticket to attend the dinner."

"Oh." She sounded disappointed. "I'm terribly sorry, Mr. Brennan, but there are no tickets available."

Better switch to Plan B. "That is unfortunate. It's such a worthwhile cause. I had planned to make a sizeable donation, but…"

He paused, waiting for Mrs. Randolph's response. He could almost hear the wheels turning. He didn't have to wait long.

"I'm not positive, of course...I'll have to check with the committee, but I'm sure we can arrange something. Shall I reserve two tickets?"

"Just one, please."

There was a short pause on the other end of the line. "You're planning to attend alone?"

"That's right."

Again, silence on the other end of the phone.

"Well, in that case, I'm sure we can accommodate you."

Jack grinned. "It will be nice to see you again, Mrs. Randolph. Perhaps you'll save me a dance or two?"

"Oh, Mr. Brennan...of course...," she sputtered. Jack could almost see her hand reaching to puff up her hair the way his mother always did when she was being complimented.

"Until Saturday, then. Goodbye."

"Goodbye."

Jack hung up the phone, a self-satisfied grin splitting his face.

Hooked. Reeled in. Landed.

* * *

Lisa was furious.

"Are you telling me that he can do this?" she asked Barry Wilson, her lawyer who'd arranged the prenuptial agreement she'd made with Carter. "How is it possible that after almost twelve years he can legally stop me from divorcing him?"

"Calm down, Lisa," Barry said sternly, although his eyes looking at her through thick lenses were kind.

Lisa collapsed in the leather chair in front of Barry's desk and shakily raked a hand through her hair. "I just can't believe he's doing this to me," she said, her mind spinning. "He's the one who dumped me, and now, just when my life is going well, he's trying to ruin it. I just don't understand him."

"You said that he wants to try again," Barry reminded her gently.

"He doesn't want me. It's a game he's playing. He just doesn't like the fact that I've gone on with my life. That's the only reason he's doing this. I know it."

"Nevertheless," Barry interjected patiently, "he is perfectly within his legal rights to contest the divorce."

"But how can he contest something that never existed—not really," Lisa cut in heatedly. "And we have divorce papers from Vegas. Doesn't that prove he didn't want to be married?"

"It does, but since those papers weren't legal..." Barry sighed. "Of course you're right. Actually, I've found in other cases that sometimes one of the partners doesn't realize how much he wants the marriage until he's faced with losing it. In my practice, it's usually been the husband who will do anything to hold on to his wife. Often, the husband has...strayed...and gotten himself caught. Now Jack, he's acting like one of those men, trying desperately to hold on to the woman he loves. Since you haven't seen him in so long, that hardly seems likely. But you never know. You say he did look for you years ago to try to re-establish a relationship, so perhaps his motives aren't entirely selfish. It's obvious that he has his reasons, and he's using every legal means at his disposal to postpone the inevitable."

Lisa rolled her eyes. "You said it."

Barry leaned forward and steepled his fingers. "But you have nothing to worry about. He'll be laughed out of court. And it'll cost him a fortune in the process. I do want to warn you that it could take time, however."

"How much time?"

"It's hard to say." Barry leaned back in his chair and looked upwards, mentally making calculations. "Normally, an uncontested divorce can be finalized relatively quickly. However, when it's a complicated case, or when one of the parties contests the action, it can take months...in some cases, years ..."

"Years!" Lisa cried. "I don't have years to wait. I'm getting married in less than a month."

Barry shook his head. "I'm sorry, Lisa, but to quote a cliché, the wheels of justice do grind slowly. I'll certainly try to expedite the proceedings, but if Jack is determined to fight the divorce, he has the advantage, since the court tends to give a married couple every opportunity to reconcile. I can't guarantee that the divorce will be granted within the next few weeks."

"Oh, no." Lisa held her breath, trying to blink back the hot, stinging tears threatening to spill over. "What am I going to do? I don't want Carter to find out about this."

Ray studied her closely. "You haven't told him?"

"No. Because...because...he wouldn't understand. He

thinks I'm so mature, so reasonable. He would never understand how impulsive I was...and his family...if it became public..."

"Hmm. I see."

Lisa's eyes flew to Barry's. "What is that supposed to mean?"

"What?"

"'Hmm, I see'".

Barry shrugged. "I'm an attorney, not a marriage counsellor, but it seems to me that a successful marriage should be built on trust and honesty. If you feel that you have to keep secrets from Carter already, then I suggest you give serious thought to whether this wedding should take place at all."

Lisa leaned forward intently. "Please don't lecture me right now, Barry. Just tell me what to do."

"You know what you should do, Lisa. You have to tell Carter."

Lisa was silent for a long moment. She could just picture the conversation. *Guess what, Carter. We'll have to postpone the wedding for a few months. I forgot to tell you that I got married eleven years ago, and we never got legally divorced. Now my husband is back, and is going to fight the divorce, because he says he wants to stay married.*

Barry smiled sympathetically at Lisa as they both stood. "One other thing. Normally, I would advise you to stay away from Jack, but if you're concerned about this issue becoming public and causing embarrassment for Carter and his family, I would suggest that it may be worthwhile to try to reason with Jack. It would be to your advantage to try to settle this amicably."

Lisa nodded resignedly. "I'll give it a try, but I doubt that he'll listen."

"Let me know if there are any new developments. In the meantime, I'll do whatever I can to expedite the matter."

"Thank you, Barry, and I'll call you. Wish me luck."

"You know I do."

Lisa laughed ruefully as she slung her purse over her shoulder. "Lord knows I need all the help I can get."

SEVEN

Lisa left Barry's office and drove to her apartment. The cloudless blue sky normally always raised her spirits, but today, even the sunshine didn't help her mood. She didn't want to speak to Jack again, didn't want to hear his voice, didn't want to remember the feel of his lips on hers.

She wrenched her thoughts away from the dangerous territory they'd wandered into and tried to concentrate on the problem she had to deal with right now. Why was he resisting the divorce? He'd said he wanted to try to mend their marriage, but that couldn't be the real reason. He couldn't still love her after all these years, could he? He didn't even really know her anymore. So what was it? What was making him do this? Vindictiveness? A cruel joke?

The icon on her phone showed that she'd had four calls while she was at the lawyer's office. She'd turned the sound off and she'd been so upset by the time her meeting with Barry was over that she'd forgotten to turn it back on when she left the building.

She clicked on the sound, then went into the kitchen, poured water into the tea kettle and set it on the stove. While the water boiled, she listened to the messages.

The first was from Carter. "Darling, I miss you. Call you later."

Lisa's stomach turned over. Guilt overwhelmed her. Guilt that she was deceiving Carter. Guilt that she'd allowed Jack to kiss her. Guilt that she'd responded to Jack's kisses in a way she'd never responded to Carter's.

The next three calls were from Jack. Just hearing his voice made her fingers tremble. It wasn't fair. No man should have a voice so smooth, so… She couldn't even come up with the right word to describe it.

Yes, she'd been ignoring his calls, avoiding the time when she'd have to speak to him again, knowing that his voice would have an effect on her. But she couldn't avoid him forever. Better to face him now and get it over with.

Before she could change her mind, she punched out his number. Her heart was pounding, her throat tight.

"Jack Brennan here."

Lisa almost hung up but forced herself not to and to speak. "It's Lisa," she croaked.

"Hi" he said. "I was just thinking about you. I wanted to apologize. I was out of line the other day, and I'm sorry. I got carried away …"

Be nice, she reminded herself. As her mother had

often said, you can attract more flies with honey than with vinegar. "You sure did," she said quietly.

"Can you forgive me if I promise to behave from now on?"

"I suppose I can."

"Thanks. I really am sorry."

"I know." He was going to take it the wrong way. She knew that, but she plowed ahead and said what she needed to say. "Jack," she began, "I have to see you."

"The gods are finally smiling down on me," he said brightly. "I knew that you couldn't resist my charm forever. Name the date, time and place. I'll be there."

"It's not what you think.".

"Sure, sweetheart," he agreed, "anything you say." Then a moment later, he added, "Sorry, I forgot you don't want me to call you sweetheart. It's a hard habit to break because that's how I've always thought of you."

Lisa was losing her temper again, and she paused to take a deep breath before she said something she would regret. "Try harder," she snapped. Then, in a softer voice, she went on. "There's something I need to talk to you about."

"We could meet at my office, or your apartment—"

"No," she said, her chest heaving. Going to Jack's office was on par with Daniel facing the lions, and as for being alone with Jack again in her apartment..."I'd prefer somewhere neutral." Somewhere public, she added silently.

"I know. I'm doing it again, aren't I?" he asked sheepishly. "I'm coming on too strong again."

"Yes you are."

"Okay, I'll try to ease up. What about lunch, then?" Jack asked. "The Garden Room. One o'clock. I'll make the reservations."

She was silent for a long time. She should refuse, but he held the upper hand. She couldn't afford to offend him, at least until she'd had the chance to explain the situation to Carter. "Fine," she finally answered, her voice quivering as she said softly, "Fine. I'll see you then."

Lisa turned into the driveway of The Garden Room at five minutes before one.

She loved the food there, and it had surprised her when Jack had suggested it. He couldn't know it was one of her favorite places to eat, and she wondered if it was one of his as well.

Two other cars were waiting to be parked when she stopped under the dark green awning, but they were whisked away and a valet opened her door for her before she had time to even check her appearance in the rear-view mirror. She got out of the car and handed her keys to the valet, then climbed the two steps to the main door where a doorman held it open for her to pass through. A silver-haired man in a tuxedo greeted her from behind the maitre d' station.

"I'm meeting Mr. Jack Brennan here," Lisa said.

The maitre d' consulted a book open on the stand. "Ah, yes," he said. "Mr. Brennan called to say he'd be a few minutes late. I'll show you to his table, though."

He turned away and Lisa followed him toward a booth shaped like a half moon. "Your server will be here momentarily," he said with a smile.

Just as he'd promised, he'd barely moved five feet away when a young woman in a white shirt, black bow tie and black skirt approached and identified herself. "May I bring you something from the bar?"

Lisa thought about it for a few seconds. She didn't usually drink anything alcoholic during the day, but under the circumstances... "A glass of white wine, please."

As the server wove her way through the tables toward the bar, Lisa's gaze drifted around the room. Tables covered with snow-white cloths dotted the space, each with a crystal vase in the center holding fresh flowers. Crystal glassware glistened in the strategic lighting and silverware gleamed.

She relaxed against the soft leather banquette, and as if by magic, the glass appeared before her. She took a sip. The wine burned her throat, but it did have the effect she had been hoping for. She immediately felt calmer, more in control...

A movement outside caught her eye, and she turned towards the plate glass window. On the pavement, a young woman was struggling with two toddlers and several shopping bags. A harried mother, obviously, yet the woman was smiling down at one of the children who was holding a plate-sized lollipop to her mouth.

Lisa smiled softly. Maybe one day...

She was so engrossed in watching the children that

she didn't notice anyone approaching until a voice whispered in her ear. "Hi," Jack whispered.

Startled, she twisted her body around to face the voice, her lips grazing Jack's cheek as he slipped into the booth beside her. She caught a whiff of peppermint-scented breath, mingling with the spicy aroma of his after-shave. Her breath came out in a gasp. "Jack."

He grinned. "What a welcome."

"Don't flatter yourself."

"You look great," he said softly.

Lisa's heart pounded and her lips still burned where they had brushed his cheek.

"Thank you," she managed. "So do you." And she meant it. He sat beside her, the picture of smooth sophistication. He was wearing a dark blue pin-striped suit, and a white dress shirt. The silk tie was patterned with small circles of red. He smiled at her, revealing a set of perfect white teeth. His smile had always been lethal, and it had only improved with age. His eyes twinkled with warmth and mischief.

Almost immediately, the server sidled seductively up to the table, and Jack turned on a dazzling smile. He ordered a scotch on the rocks, and Lisa asked for a glass of Chardonnay.

"Do you still always order steak when you go out for dinner?" has asked once the server hurried away.

Lisa chuckled. "It's my go-to. I've never been able to cook it as well at home."

"Baked potato and salad?"

She nodded.

"Do you mind if I order for you?" he asked as the server approached with their drinks on a silver tray.

"Not at all," Lisa replied.

The server set the drinks on the table and asked if they needed more time to look at the menus.

Jack smiled at the young woman. "No," he said. "I'd like your best steak, please...for my wife..." he glanced pointedly at Lisa, "and the same for me. Baked potatoes and Caesar salad with extra garlic."

Jack winked at the awestruck girl frantically making notes in her book, and added, "But bring some after-dinner mints as well. I might want to give my wife a kiss..."

The server giggled and left.

"Why did you say that?" Lisa demanded. "Of all the unmitigated gall—"

"What did I say? You aren't upset because I told a waitress that you're my wife."

"I most certainly am upset," she said heatedly. "And I'm not your wife, at least not in the real sense of the word."

"Not yet, but I really hope that one day you'll come to your senses and you will be," Jack took Lisa's hand in his. "And I do want to kiss my wife—"

"What you want and what you get are two different things."

"I'm hoping that you're going to change your mind, and that what I want and what I get will be one and the same."

Lisa's throat felt thick, clogged with confused emotion, and forming coherent words suddenly seemed beyond her means. To avoid saying something idiotic, she gulped the remainder of her wine, gasping as the liquid seared her throat.

Jack laughed then, a rich, deep laugh.

She couldn't help herself. She'd never been able to resist his laugh without laughing herself. And even though she tried, she couldn't prevent her lips twitching. "Jack," she said, pulling her hand away from his. "Please be serious. I need to talk to you."

A frown crossed Jack's face and his mouth pursed. The effect was more comical than serious. "Is this better?"

"Jack, I mean it," Lisa's voice was louder than usual, and curious glances turned in her direction from the surrounding tables.

"Lisa," he said, his face splitting into a grin, "you need to relax. Let's just have a pleasant lunch. Then we'll talk. Honest. I don't believe in mixing good food with unpleasant words."

She shook her head in undisguised frustration. Why couldn't he understand that she didn't want to have a pleasant lunch with him? Every moment she spent in his company brought out old familiar but involuntary sensations in the pit of her stomach, as well as other feelings she'd rather not think about. Every time she looked at his face, her eyes slipped downwards to his lips, the lips that had pressed against hers ...

Her face flamed at the unbidden memory. "Fine, Jack," she said shortly. "We'll have a pleasant lunch."

She sat stonily as the server placed their meals on the table. "Is there anything else you'd like?" she asked.

Jack gazed at Lisa boldly. "There sure is," he whispered, "but I'm a patient man. I can wait." His eyes never left Lisa's face, and the server smiled knowingly. Lisa looked away in embarrassment.

Jack's good humor was contagious, and even though she tried to fight it, before she knew it, Lisa was explaining how she had happened to find herself in the hotel business, and how she and Carter had met and fallen in love.

"The hospitality industry suits you perfectly," Jack commented later as they dipped into a dessert of brandied cherries and ice cream.

"It really does," Lisa agreed, her eyes sparkling. "But I must admit that when I graduated from college, my dream was to own a small inn somewhere near a lake, or the ocean. A dozen rooms or so, a pool, maybe a tennis court and a couple of horses for guests. A home-away-from-home type of hotel. Large hotel chains are fine for corporate-minded people, but they are so impersonal that I never get a chance to even meet the guests."

"So why don't you?"

"Why don't I what?"

"Invest in a bed-and-breakfast," Jack said intently. "Follow your dream. Or has Carter forbidden it?"

"Of course not. Carter doesn't..." A slow blush crept across Lisa's face. She wasn't about to tell Jack that she had never mentioned her dream to Carter, that in one lunch she had opened up more to Jack than she had ever done with Carter.

"Carter doesn't what?" Jack prodded.

"Carter doesn't tell me what to do. He lets me make my own decisions."

"Hmm. He 'lets' you, does he?" Jack muttered. "Well, isn't that nice of him."

The conversation was taking a turn for the worse. "Can we get to the purpose of this meeting now that you've had lunch?"

"Sure thing. By the looks of your face, though, you're the bearer of bad news."

"I want you to reconsider contesting the divorce," she said in a tight, controlled voice.

"No."

"You're wasting your time."

"No," he repeated.

"You're going to lose in the end anyway, and it'll cost you a fortune, so what do you hope to gain by dragging it through the courts?"

He stared at her in silence for what seemed a long time before he answered. "Time. Time to win you back. And I'll do anything I have to do to get that time."

"You can't seriously think that we're ever going to be husband and wife again."

"But I do. And once you get used to the idea, and you realize that you still love me as much as I still love you, it'll be just like we planned it the day we got married."

"You have a high opinion of yourself, don't you?" Lisa retorted. "I happen to be in love with Carter. We're going to be married. That's a fact. And I will never, repeat never, be your wife again, in any way."

Jack grinned his devilish smile. "Never say never.

Words have a way of coming back to haunt you. I happen to recall a time when you said you would never spend a night in my bed—"

"That's not fair—"

"But true," he pointed out. "And if I remember correctly, I didn't have to drag you into it, either."

"I...anyway, that was then. And stalling the divorce isn't going to do you any good. You're being stubborn, but that shouldn't surprise me. You always were the most obstinate—" she began.

"Not obstinate. Patient. Only one of my more endearing qualities, or so I've been told."

A slow blush crept over Lisa's face. In the first few days of their marriage, Lisa had often commented on the extent of Jack's patience.

"Remember?"

Lisa groaned and took a sip of the coffee at her elbow while she considered her next move. She didn't have one.

She raised her hand for the server to bring the check."

"I've got it," Jack said.

"Fine." She stood up and slung her purse over her shoulder. "Obviously, some things never change. You are still the immature, stubborn, self-centered jock I knew in high school." She leaned toward Jack, bracing herself with her hands gripping the edge of the table. "Go ahead, then. Contest the divorce. Make a fool of yourself. But I can guarantee that you will never be my husband again. I don't make the same mistakes twice."

She straightened. "Thanks for lunch," she spat out as she spun around and headed toward the front doors.

"You're welcome," she heard him say. "And like I said before, never say never, sweetheart. You're going to have to eat those words one day soon."

A blast of icy wind hit her when she stepped out onto the sidewalk. As she passed by the plate glass window, she couldn't resist the temptation to look and see what he was doing now. Probably flirting with the waitress, she mused. She glanced inside, and there he was, actually grinning at her.

He'd known she would look back, that her curiosity wouldn't let her walk away without taking one last peek at him. Had she changed so little over the years that he could predict exactly what she would say and do? As she made her way back to the hotel, she wondered if he really did know her better than she knew herself.

EIGHT

Lisa was nursing a cup of coffee at the kitchen table in her sister's compact bungalow the next afternoon when she heard the front door open. Sunshine peeked through the bare branches of the birch tree outside the window, and Lisa gazed absently at the stark silhouette the tree made against the brilliant blue sky.

"Larry? Are you home?" Karen, Lisa's younger sister called out from the other side of the house.

"In the kitchen," Lisa replied. Moments later, a ball of fluff reminding Lisa of an overgrown snowball barrelled into the kitchen and pounced at Lisa, pushing her back into the chair. Lisa chuckled as a very long, very pink tongue lapped at her face.

Her attention was so absorbed by the over-affectionate animal that she didn't see or hear anyone approaching until four arms grabbed her neck from behind and began to squeeze. "Hey, Auntie Li," two small voices cried out in unison. "We didn't know you was here."

"Tyler! Kevin! Enough!" A slender, dark-haired woman came into the kitchen. "You're strangling your aunt! And take Scooter into the yard."

The two boys glanced at each other, then gradually released their grip and dragged the wriggling puppy off Lisa's lap. "We was just givin' her a hug. And so was Scooter."

"And a great hug it was, too." Lisa grinned at the two boys standing beside her, both so alike with their sand-coloured hair and freckles.

"Have you been here long? I didn't know you were coming." Karen was busy brushing long white strands of fur from Lisa's black wool jacket hanging over the back of the chair. "If I'd realized you were here, I'd have kept the dog on his leash. I don't know why, but he seems to go crazy whenever he sees you."

"That's because he knows I'm a soft touch for a cold nose and a wagging tail," Lisa said with a smile.

"Where's Larry?" Karen asked, glancing around the empty kitchen.

"He's gone next door for a few minutes. I hope you don't mind. I made myself at home. There's coffee on the stove ..."

"Uh, sure ..." Karen glanced around, almost as if she was in unfamiliar surroundings instead of her own kitchen.

"Is something wrong?" Lisa asked. The tell-tale sign

was there, Karen chewing on her bottom lip. It was a habit she'd developed when they were youngsters, and whenever she was nervous or upset, she nibbled on it. Once or twice over the years, she'd even made it bleed.

"No. Why?"

"I know you," Lisa said with a soft smile. "Something's going on. What's up?" As she voiced the question, Lisa couldn't help wondering whether she would regret asking. Karen's life seemed to be in a constant state of crisis. One of the six-year-old twins was either trying to see if sticking his fingers in an electric socket would make him light up, or the other was trying to imitate Superman by flying from his bedroom window to the tree outside, two floors up.

Karen dropped into the kitchen chair across the table from Lisa and heaped a spoonful of sugar into a mug of steaming coffee. Aha, Lisa thought, another sign. Karen was constantly watching her weight. "Do you remember Jim Vickers, Larry's roommate when he was in college?"

Lisa nodded. She'd met him a few times, first at Karen's wedding, and then at the twins' baptism. She remembered him as being huge, tanned and outdoorsy. Rather good-looking, in a rugged sort of way, but a little too blustery for her taste.

"Well," Karen went on, "he called Jim the other day. Jim and three other friends of his have bought a marina on Lake Champlain and he's asked Larry to be the third partner."

Lisa's knowledge of geography consisted of what she'd learned in school. "Isn't that in Canada?"

Karen shook her head. "No…well, part of it is, but the most of it is in New York." She took a sip of her coffee. "He's so excited, Lisa, but I really have my doubts."

Lisa whistled softly. "That's quite a decision to make."

"It means giving up his job and moving up there, and if it doesn't work out…"

Karen's words faded, but Lisa knew what thoughts were running through her mind. Flashes of their childhood, years of wearing hand-me-down clothes from the neighbors, never being able to attend after-school activities, doing without. Years and years of doing without.

"Larry has a good job here, secure, and we've started to put money away for the twins' education."

"Hasn't Larry has always wanted to live in the country and be his own boss?"

"That's the problem. He has. And it sounds wonderful," Karen murmured. "The property has a dozen cabins, a repair shop, and they're planning to rent snowmobiles in the winter and groom trails for cross-country skiing. In the summer, they have boats for rent as well as fishing tackle and bait. The owner's retiring."

"It sounds like a great opportunity."

"It does, doesn't it? But I'm so scared, Lisa. It means risking everything. We've worked so hard to get what we have, I'm afraid to take the chance of losing it."

Lisa understood how badly a person could be hurt by taking risks. Hadn't she taken a huge risk by falling in love with a boy from the other side of the tracks? She'd lost, but maybe Karen and Larry wouldn't.

"If this is what will make you happy, then you have to do it. If you don't, you'll regret it for the rest of your life. Don't settle for anything less, Karen."

"I know you're right, but—"

"I *am* right. Promise me you'll think about this with an open mind."

Karen nodded. "I will."

"If you do decide to go, I'll miss you like crazy, but you have to do what's right for you and your family." Lisa leaned back in her chair and sipped her coffee. If only she had the courage to follow her own advice.

"Jim's asked Larry to spend a few days up there the week after next to meet the other partners and look around."

"And he wants to go." It was a statement, not a question. Knowing Larry, he already had his bags packed.

Karen nodded. "He wants to do this so badly, but like I said, it's a huge risk. We'd be gambling everything we own, and we could lose everything."

Lisa studied the coffee in her mug. She could understand Karen's reluctance, but she also knew how much Larry enjoyed the outdoors, and how talented he was with machines and motors. Even though he'd gone to college, he wasn't completely happy unless he was under a car or tinkering with a motor of some kind. "Then what are you going to do?" she asked finally, grateful that it wasn't her decision to make.

"He'd like to go, and I told him to, but he won't go if I'm not comfortable with the idea."

Lisa wasn't surprised. Karen and Larry's relationship had never ceased to amaze the family. When Karen was nineteen, she had gone on a cruise with a friend, returned with Larry, married him three months later and they were still blissfully happy.

Money was tight, and there were few luxuries, especially after the arrival of twin boys less than a year later. But the babies had only strengthened the bond. They spent every minute together and hated to be separated.

At the time, Lisa had been trying to deal with her own broken heart, and had been forced to admit that she'd envied her sister. Although she'd been happy for her, she'd gone through quite a poor-me period, wondering why she couldn't have the same happiness. But that had passed, and Lisa's envy had disappeared. Karen had never wanted to have a career, and with Larry, she seemed to have what she wanted—a husband, a home, and children.

Lisa heard the front door open. "I'm back," Larry called out, "but I'll be in the garage for a while."

"Okay," Karen shouted out. "Don't be too long. Dinner will be ready soon."

"Why don't you go with him and look around?" Lisa suggested after the front door slammed shut behind Larry. "You might be able to think about it more clearly once you've seen the area and you know all the details."

"Well...I suppose you're right. But it's business. I don't think it would be fair to take the twins when they can't have any freedom." She gave Lisa a wry grin, "You know how they are."

Lisa chuckled. Yes, she knew exactly how they were, rambunctious, curious, adorable little boys who couldn't manage to sit still for more than five minutes.

Karen glanced around and cocked her head to the side, listening for the sound of the twins' voices in another room. "You know," she whispered, "this is the first time, and probably the last, that I sort of regret having children, although I feel as if a fork of lightning should strike me down for saying such a thing. I wouldn't really trade the boys for anything in the world."

"I'm sure everyone feels that way now and then, Karen," Lisa offered in sympathy.

"I suppose so. It's just that it would be terrific to have a few days alone, just the two of us, but…"

Without hesitation, Lisa spoke up. "I'll keep the twins."

A short laugh exploded out of Karen. She looked at Lisa intently as if she had lost her mind. "Nothing personal, Lisa," her sister began, "but you don't know anything about kids, particularly six-year-old boys with a death wish."

"What's to know?" Lisa questioned confidently. "Surely I can manage to keep two little boys healthy and safe for a few days. They've stayed with me before and I've returned them without more than a few bumps and bruises."

"Aren't you too busy?" Karen questioned. "What about the wedding plans? And the opening of the hotel? Won't you be tied up with the ribbon-cutting and the parties?"

At the mention of the wedding, Lisa's heart jolted. There would be no wedding until the mess with Jack was settled, but she didn't want to go into that now. She would sort through that later, after Karen's second honeymoon was organized. Karen had enough on her mind without worrying about Lisa's problems as well.

"The wedding plans are under control," she lied. "As for the opening of Randolph Place, I'm not really involved with that. You aren't leaving until the day after, right?"

Karen nodded.

"Good. I can do a lot of the paperwork at home in the evenings. That's not a problem. I'll drop the boys off at school in the morning and pick them up in the afternoon. Besides," she added, "it's only a few days."

"I don't know…"

Lisa could see how Karen was torn between her desire to spend a few days alone with her husband, and her concern for the safety of her boys.

Lisa grinned. "Then it's settled. Go right now and tell Larry to get ready for his second honeymoon."

Karen blushed and giggled, lowering her voice to a whisper. "We're still on the first one, if you know what I mean." She got up and walked over to the doorway separating the kitchen from the rest of the house.

She looked back over her shoulder at Lisa. "Are you sure?" she asked one last time.

"Positive."

Beaming, Karen disappeared around the corner into the living room. A few minutes later, she returned, eyes sparkling.

"It's arranged. Larry's so happy. Thank you, Lisa. You have no idea what this means to us."

For the next hour, the two women discussed Karen's forthcoming weekend and made arrangements for the care of the twins. Lisa was on her third cup of coffee when the back door opened and the boys bounded in.

"Tyler, Kevin," Karen said, placing one arm around each boy's shoulder and drawing them close to her. "How would you feel about spending some time with Aunt Lisa?"

"At her house?" Tyler asked.

Karen nodded.

"Just us?" Kevin prodded. "Without you or Daddy?"

"That's right. Just you and Tyler and me," Lisa said, crouching down to a face-to-face level with the boys.

"Yippee!" they cried in unison. Suddenly, Tyler grabbed Kevin's arm and whispered something to him. The smiles disappeared and they both regarded each other intently before Kevin turned to Lisa.

"What about the man?"

"What man?"

"The man with the suitcase? The one who was at your house the last time we were there?"

Lisa smiled. "Oh, you mean Mr. Randolph."

Kevin nodded. "Yeah, that's him. Will he be there?"

"He'll be visiting occasionally. Why?"

Kevin pressed his face to Lisa's ear. He was trying to whisper, but his voice was loud enough for everyone to hear. "We don't like him."

"Kevin," Karen scolded. "That's not a very nice thing to say."

"Well, we don't. And he doesn't like us," Tyler said loudly, reinforcing his brother's opinion. "I heard him tell Auntie Lisa that he didn't like us being there 'cause we're too stricking. Didn't he, Kev?"

Kevin nodded adamantly in his mother's direction while Karen gave Lisa an apologetic glance.

Out of the mouth of babes, Lisa thought as she watched the exchange between Karen and the twins. Lisa couldn't remember Carter had ever actually saying that he didn't like children, and Lisa was convinced that once he had his own child to love, he would be an adoring father, just like Larry was. After all, how could any man not love his children?

But what was 'stricking'? Obviously the twins had overheard Carter when they had spent the weekend a few months ago, but she couldn't remember every word that had passed between them.

"Kevin," Lisa pressed, "do you remember exactly what Mr. Randolph said?"

For a few seconds, Kevin stared at the wall behind Lisa, his forehead wrinkled in concentration. Then, as if a light had suddenly gone on, he said, "He said we're stricking."

"But what else did he say?" Lisa prodded. If the boys could remember the context of the conversation, perhaps she could find out what 'stricking' was.

Kevin shrugged. Then Tyler interrupted "You and him was fighting, 'cause he wanted to go out and you didn't."

Lisa remembered that argument. The twins were watching television in the spare bedroom while she and Carter were working at the dining table. Carter had made reservations for dinner at an exclusive restaurant without telling her first, and Lisa had refused to hire a sitter for the boys. Carter had been miffed, and had made the comment the boys had heard, that children were too restricting, not 'stricking'.

"Carter and I weren't fighting, we were having a discussion. And I'm sure Carter likes you. He was just hungry, and when he's hungry, he gets grumpy."

"Me too," Tyler chimed in. "Daddy says I'm like an old bear when I'm hungry."

Lisa laughed, and the boys broke into grins and began to giggle. "Hey, Auntie Lisa, can we sleep in the big bed, and watch TV in bed, and go to the park, and the zoo, and ..."

"Hold it, you two," Karen interrupted. "Aunt Lisa has work to do, so she may not have time to take you to the zoo. You'll have to wait and see. If you're really good, though, she might. That is, if the zoo is open."

With the prospect of a visit to the zoo, the twins whooped and yahooed and raced out of the kitchen and up the stairs. Lisa cringed at the sound of their footsteps overhead. "It sounds like an earthquake," she said, laughing.

Karen grinned knowingly at Lisa. "You'll be sorry. I guarantee that by the time I get back, you'll need a vacation."

Lisa's mood had brightened considerably by the time she backed her Lexus out of her sister's driveway and headed back to the city. She was looking forward to having the twins with her, and even though they were rambunctious and noisy, they were normal little boys and she loved them dearly.

The next few days would be exceptionally busy, but with some rescheduling of meetings, and working a few extra hours between now and the weekend, she would be able to take some time to spend with the children.

May as well get some work done now, she thought as she headed down the freeway toward the city.

The hotel lobby was a picture of understated elegance, as always, yet it seemed barren now that the Christmas decorations had been taken down and packed away. Lisa crossed to the front desk, her trained eye taking in every detail, making a mental note to replace a couple of the potted plants near the elevator.

"Good evening, Miss McKenzie," the concierge said, glancing up from his desk. "It's rather late. Is everything all right?"

"Good evening, George," she replied, smiling at the balding man with the frown creasing his forehead. "Everything's fine. Just catching up on some unfinished work."

The concierge nodded gravely, then turned his attention back to his work. I wonder if he has ever had a really good belly laugh, she mused as the elevator rose to the executive suites on the top floor. Somehow she doubted it.

The concierge's sense of humor—or lack of it—was quickly forgotten as Lisa sat down at her desk and began to sort through the stack of work waiting for her. By the time she glanced at her watch again, it was after midnight.

She rose from her desk and stretched, trying to ease the tightness in her shoulders and neck. Slowly, she crossed to the window and gazed out at the twinkling lights of the city below her. It never ceased to amaze her that behind those lights, in every apartment building, house and office complex, there were people who had problems, some much worse than hers.

But even though her situation with Jack wasn't life-threatening, it was still a serious problem, and it preyed on her mind. Her attorney's words came back to haunt her—'tell Carter', 'marriage should be built on trust and honesty'.

He was right. Lisa knew that. And she'd been foolish to keep her marriage a secret from Carter. She'd been silly to think he'd never find out, when all it would take would be a chance meeting with someone from her past.

Saturday. I'll tell him on Saturday. But I'll tell him after the dance. There's no point in ruining his evening sooner than I have to.

Once she'd decided on a course of action, she could feel the tension release. Fatigue took its place, and she yawned. Time to call it a night, she thought, as she picked up her coat and purse and left her office.

Jack rolled over and glanced at the clock beside his bed. Three-twenty-two. He threw off the blankets and tumbled out of bed, swearing at the inconsiderate numbers on the alarm clock. Lord, he had to get some sleep before he turned into a zombie.

Every night since he'd seen Lisa's face on television, he'd fallen asleep only to dream about her in his arms, kissing him, loving him…

He couldn't go on like this, he realized, switching on the light in the bathroom and turning on the cold water faucet. He'd taken more cold showers in the last few days than he had all during his teen years.

What was he going to do about her? He was already doing the only thing he could by contesting the divorce. His attorney had almost laughed out loud when he'd consulted him about his legal options.

"Don't be a fool," he'd told Jack, "you don't have a leg to stand on. No judge in his right mind is going to take your side."

"I realize that," Jack conceded, "but it's the only thing I can do to stall for time while I try to convince her that Randolph isn't the guy for her."

The attorney ran his finger down a list of figures on a piece of paper. "Is it worth what it's going to cost?"

Jack nodded. "It's worth every cent I have."

"It may cost you exactly that by the time this is over."

Jack had left his attorney's office holding on to the man's promise to pull out all the stops, to use every legal loophole and precedent he could find to postpone the court's final decision.

All Jack had to do now was wait...but waiting, without doing, wasn't something Jack was very good at.

NINE

By Saturday evening, Lisa was exhausted. Long hours at the hotel had taken their toll, and she was well aware that the tight knot of tension in the back of her head was due to her anxiety about her forthcoming confession to Carter. She would be very lucky if she got through the night with less than an all-out migraine attack.

This evening was important to Carter and his family, and Lisa had spent weeks searching for the perfect gown. She'd spent more than she wanted to, but as she slipped into the strapless gown, she knew it had been worth every penny. She twirled in front of the full-length mirror on the back of her bedroom door and grinned. She was more than pleased with the results of her day of primping. She looked fabulous, she admitted to herself. She'd never looked so sophisticated, but at the same time she felt…sexy.

The gown itself was simply styled, a creation of

aquamarine silk fabric that clung to her curves and floated downward in varying shades of blue. With every step she took, the skirt shimmered, reminding Lisa of the waves in a tropical sea. She'd decided against jewellery except for the diamond bracelet Carter had given her as a Christmas gift, and the small diamond clasp in her hair.

She was touching up her lips with rose lipstick when the buzzer rang. Right on time naturally, she mused, as she glanced at the clock.

Happily, she opened the door to admit Carter. The smile on his face disappeared as his eyes slowly appraised her. He stood in the hallway, staring open-mouthed as Lisa moved toward him. "Welcome back, Carter," she breathed.

"I...ah...you look...that's quite a dress..."

Lisa felt herself flush. "Thank you. I bought it in a small boutique near the hotel. I'd almost given up ever finding just the right dress for tonight when I happened to see it as I walked past the store one day."

"Is there a jacket or something to wear over it?" Carter asked.

"No," Lisa replied hesitantly. "Why?"

"Oh, no reason..." he said, "it's just so...so..." He waved his hands in the air, as if the movement could explain the words that he was having so much trouble coming up with.

"So what, Carter?" Lisa's pleasure vanished. He was looking at her as if he'd never seen her before, and the expression on his face was definitely not one of approval. She'd been so sure he would be pleased with her choice. She'd thought he would compliment her, not stare at her as if he was almost...embarrassed.

Lisa noticed the slight tinge in his cheeks, and he swallowed awkwardly before he spoke, almost as if he was trying to choose just the right words. "Are you sure it's appropriate...I mean...it's quite...sexy...I didn't think...that is, you don't usually wear such...the guests this evening are so...conservative .."

What was the matter with her? Of course he was shocked; he had every reason to be. Her wardrobe, until this particular purchase, consisted of tailored suits and simple dresses, and even when she was attending social functions, she tended to stay with modest rather than decorative or flattering outfits.

"I'm not exactly nude, you know," Lisa grumbled softly, suddenly feeling a little miffed. She had so expected him to be—what? What exactly had she expected from him? That he would take one look at her and break into a wolf-whistle? Hardly. "You're so stuffy sometimes," she blurted out without thinking.

As soon as the words left her mouth, Lisa regretted them. Shock registered on Carter's face, and Lisa wished she could bite off her tongue.

But it was true. She hadn't realized before now just how restricted Carter's life was. Restrained, discreet, the model of appropriate behavior. In the time they'd been together, she'd never seen him with a hair out of place, and for the first time since they'd met, she had an overwhelming urge to run her fingers through it and muss it up. She smiled softly at the thought of how he would react if she did just that.

He'd think she'd lost her mind. It might be worth it, though, she thought wickedly, just to see what would happen.

This was all Jack's fault, she thought angrily. It was Jack who was filling her head with doubts. Doubts that had never entered her head before. And now here she was not only having doubts, but actually voicing them.

"I realize you're clothed," Carter conceded, "but barely." He smiled at her, as if that would take the bite out of his words, but he failed. Suddenly she felt dirty, as if her appearance was somehow indecent. "I mean…" he went on, "isn't that more for an intimate evening alone…"

Lisa couldn't believe her ears, and for a moment, she considered going into the bedroom and changing her dress. The moment passed, replaced by anger. Her dress had cost a fortune, and even if it was a little more daring than she normally wore, she felt wonderful in it.

"This is the dress I'm wearing," Lisa said brightly, crossing the living room to pick up her wrap and evening bag from the chair beside the door. "Shall we go?"

Carter checked his watch. "Very well," he muttered. "There's no time to change now anyway. If we don't hurry, we'll be late."

"Fine," Lisa muttered, feeling the knot in her head tighten just a little more.

Rain was beginning to fall as Carter escorted Lisa to his Porsche and she slipped inside. The drive to the hotel was silent, except for the soft purr of the engine and the rhythmic squeak of the wipers cleaning the windshield. After almost a week of being separated from each other, their reunion should have been happy, filled with words of love and longing. Instead, they'd treated each other more like polite strangers.

She remembered when Jack had gone for two days to the college for a campus tour, every minute seemed like an eternity. And when he got back, they couldn't keep their hands off each other. It was as if he'd been gone for months.

Lisa gasped involuntarily, and Carter quickly shot a worried glance in her direction. "What's wrong?"

Lisa shook her head. "Nothing...a cramp in my toe," she lied. What was the matter with her? Ever since her lunch with Jack, memories of their times together kept popping into her brain at the most inconvenient times. Whenever she thought of Carter, for some reason, Jack's face appeared, and his low, sexy voice spoke Carter's words.

"The weatherman is calling for heavy rain later tonight," Lisa said, breaking the silence.

"Mmm."

"And tomorrow," she added.

"Uh-huh."

Lisa gave up and stared out the window until the car stopped under the hotel canopy. Tom, a valet she'd hired a few months before, rushed to open her door. "Wow, Miss McKenzie," he gushed once she'd gotten out. "You're a real knockout." Then, apparently noticing the disparaging looks he was receiving from his employer, he stuttered, "Uh...sorry...I didn't mean..."

Lisa grinned, her spirits reviving. At least somebody thought she was attractive. It should have been Carter who noticed, though, not the valet.

"That's all right, Tom," she replied with a soft smile. "And thank you for the compliment," she added as she took Carter's arm and allowed him to usher her through the crowds and paparazzi who were crawling all over each other trying to catch a glimpse of the celebrities pulling up at the curb. Flashbulbs popped around her, blinding her momentarily, but for the most part, the photographers ignored their arrival, and they quickly escaped through the revolving doors into the hotel.

Several people were already milling around when they entered the ballroom. Waiters carrying trays of hors d'oeuvres deftly and silently wove their way through the guests. Lisa smiled and greeted those she knew as she made her way across the room to where Carter's parents and his sister were having cocktails.

"Good evening, Lisa. It's wonderful to see you again." Eleanor Randolph smiled, but the smile didn't reach her eyes. Her tone contradicted the affectionate words.

Just like Jack's mother, she thought. She didn't think I was good enough for her son either.

"Hello, Mrs. Randolph. Mr. Randolph," Lisa said to the distinguished-looking grey-haired man sitting beside Carter's mother.

"Nice to see you, Lisa." Carter's father greeted her with a smile.

At least he seemed to mean it, she thought.

"And please call me Devon," he went on. "After all, we're going to be family. Now sit down and let me get you both a drink."

Devon disappeared among the tuxedo-clad men hovering near the bar. Lisa smiled at Carter's sister, looking very bored. "How are you, Susan?" she asked.

Susan shrugged and looked away.

Carter was deep in conversation with his mother and two recent arrivals, leaving Lisa to survey the other occupants of the room.

Compared to some of the other guests, Lisa didn't think her choice of dress had been so outrageous after all. A woman who Lisa recognized, the wife of a well-known local sports figure, was wearing an ultra-modern sequined miniskirt and top, her midriff bare, and flaunting every curve God had given her. And probably some her plastic surgeon had given her, too, she thought.

She felt her lips tug in a wry smile. Carter should be thankful she hadn't worn an outfit like that. She could just imagine the look on his face if she'd opened the door to greet him dressed in a miniskirt and her breasts barely contained. He would have had a coronary right on the spot.

Actually, cruel as it seemed, he needed to be shaken up a little bit. It would probably be good for him.

Oh, no! She was starting to think like Jack. And that was the last thing she wanted to do.

She turned her attention to Carter's sister, staring sullenly at the wine glass she was twirling in her hands. "How's school, Susan? Are you enjoying it?"

Carter's younger sister was currently a student at a university in New York, so Lisa hadn't had a chance to really get to know her well. The few times they'd met, Susan seemed unhappy, but Lisa had no idea why.

"Sure. It's a barrel of laughs."

"An education is never wasted—"

"Spare me, Lisa," Susan interrupted. "Do you really think I need to learn about marketing and macro-economics?"

"Well…"

"Am I ever going to have to support myself?"

"You never know," Lisa put in.

"Do you think men are interested in my brains?" She laughed, a bitter sound. "Men are interested in me for one thing, my family's money. They wouldn't care if I couldn't add two and two together. I found that out the hard way."

That one sentence explained Susan's attitude. Carter had been hurt the same way, by someone who'd pretended to love him, but had used him only for the prestige and wealth associated with him.

"Not everyone is interested in money," Lisa said. "There are other things, more important things—"

"Well," Susan interrupted, "once you and brother dear are married, you won't have to worry about money. Then you can concentrate on those *important* things."

"I don't worry about money now. I've never had it, and I don't miss it. Carter and I concentrate on things like respect, and trust, and companionship."

"Sure, like you'd want him if he worked in a factory,

or dug ditches for a living?"

"Yes I would," Lisa insisted. "Your brother is a wonderful man who'll make an equally wonderful husband. You have the wrong idea, Susan. Money can give you luxury, but it can also ruin your life and destroy relationships."

Through the sullen expression, Susan looked slightly intrigued. "How can having money ruin your life?"

Lisa was tempted to tell her exactly how money had shattered her dreams, but she stopped herself.

Easy! I thought I'd met the right man once. If he'd been dirt poor, we'd probably still be married today and have a houseful of kids. But his family was wealthy. It didn't matter to me where we lived, or if we had to scrub floors to earn a living, as long as we were together. But he didn't give me the chance to tell him that. He made the decision for me...and broke my heart.

"Don't let money affect your decisions, Susan. And when you find the right man, you'll realize that his occupation, or how rich he is, doesn't really matter."

A slow glimmer of a smile appeared on Susan's face as she began to stare at something behind Lisa. "Whaddayaknow, I think I just found him."

Lisa turned and followed Susan's gaze, then froze. There, standing in profile at the other side of the room, was Jack.

The faint pounding in Lisa's head suddenly felt more like a bass drum in a pipe band.

"Hey, what's the matter?" Susan's voice seemed

vague, distant. Lisa tore her gaze away from Jack and glanced at Susan. "Nothing. I..."

"Good. 'Cause by the look I saw on your face, seemed to me maybe you were deciding to dump brother dear and set your sights on somebody with even more money. But you can forget it. I saw him first."

Lisa nodded absently as Susan picked up her wine glass and sauntered across the room toward Jack and his companions, swaying her hips suggestively.

Lisa watched her go, a thousand thoughts swirling in her brain. What was Jack doing here? Why hadn't he told her? What if he said something...mentioned their marriage...he didn't know she hadn't told Carter yet...

"Here you are, my dear." Carter's father appeared at Lisa's elbow and handed her a glass of wine.

"Thank you," she croaked, taking the glass and gulping down half the contents, trying to quench the sudden dryness in her throat.

Devon glanced at the glass then curiously up at her. "I believe we're to take our seats now," he said, indicating several people heading towards the dais at the far end of the room. "It appears that we're seated right beside each other. I'm a lucky man."

Lisa grinned. She liked Carter's father, and genuinely enjoyed his company. She said a silent thankyou to whoever had planned the seating arrangements. Perhaps she'd get through this night after all.

"How are plans progressing for the opening?" Devon asked as he held her chair for her. "I haven't had a chance to speak to Carter since he got back."

The hotel...right. "Right on schedule," she replied. The conversation quickly turned to a discussion of the latest developments concerning the opening of the new hotel, and to general management problems. After a few appropriate remarks, Lisa remained silent.

Knowing that Jack was somewhere behind her, perhaps watching her, made her uneasy. Dinner tasted like sawdust, and Lisa could choke back only a few bites before she gave up.

As soon as the dessert plates were cleared, Carter's mother took the podium and gave a short speech, thanking the guests for their generosity.

"She's quite a woman," Devon whispered to Lisa as Eleanor stepped down from the dais and crossed the room toward them.

"She certainly is." A faint smile tugged at her lips. She was sure she and Devon didn't mean it in the same way.

As Eleanor took her seat, a small orchestra began to play, and couples gradually filled the dance floor.

Lisa couldn't help herself. She casually shifted so she could see the dance floor and caught a glimpse of Jack and Susan near a wall of French doors leading out to a patio.

Susan was leaning into him, her arms wrapped so tightly around his neck there wasn't an inch of space between them.

A knot formed in Lisa's stomach. At least he seemed to be doing his best to keep his distance, but at the same time, he was giving Susan that devastatingly sexy smile, the one that had always turned he knees to jelly.

Who cares? Lisa thought, turning away. It didn't matter to her if Susan seduced Jack. Susan could have him. So why did the sight of Jack holding Susan in his arms and the thought of them making love later fill her with this incredible sense of fury, and overwhelming pain?

Was it because, even though she had fought against it for almost a dozen years, she still cared about him? Or was it just her being childish, and that even though she didn't want Jack, she didn't want anyone else to have him? Especially Susan, the spoiled brat.

TEN

The music faded, and Susan came back to the table. Behind her was Jack, holding her hand. At least he had the good sense to look guilty.

"Look who I found, Mother," she announced.

"Mr. Brennan," Eleanor gushed. "It's so nice to see you again. How long has it been? A year?"

What? They knew each other. That meant he probably knew Carter, too. Why didn't he tell me he knew Carter? Jerk.

"And you, Mrs. Randolph," he replied, pressing a kiss to the back of her hand in a grand Continental gesture. "You look ravishing, as usual."

Eleanor beamed. "I'm so glad I was able to round up an extra ticket for you. It's difficult at the last minute—"

"I'm sure it is. Believe me, I do appreciate it," he replied.

Jack went behind her to where Carter and his father

were sitting. Both men stood up when he approached. "Devon. Carter." He nodded towards the two men and held out his hand. Carter took it and pumped it vigorously. "Good to see you," he said. "I hope you're enjoying yourself."

Lisa wished she could crawl under the table and disappear when his eyes met hers. "I'd like to introduce my fiancé, Lisa McKenzie. Jack Brennan," Carter said.

Lisa opened her mouth to speak, but the words refused to form.

Jack turned back to Carter. "Lisa and I..." he began, his eyes still on hers.

Lisa pleaded with him with her eyes, and by the subtle change in his expression, she knew he understood.

"...are old friends. We knew each other in high school," he finished, a grin splitting his face. "In fact, I stopped by the hotel a few days ago to say hello. Didn't she tell you?"

Carter's eyes narrowed slightly, as if he were trying to decide whether to accept Jack's explanation or not. He hesitated before he replied but finally smiled. "Yes, she did mention something about a surprise visitor. Of course I had no idea it was you."

"She got quite a shock," he said to Carter, then turned towards her. Lisa noticed the teasing glint in his eye, and the devilish grin. "Didn't you, Lisa?"

Still the words stuck in her throat. She nodded numbly.

"Do you mind if I have a dance with your fiancé, Carter?" Jack questioned. "For old times' sake?"

Carter smiled graciously, but Lisa noted the hidden current of tension in his words. "Not at all."

"Lisa?" Jack's eyebrows lifted.

How could she refuse without raising questions? She couldn't, so she just smiled graciously and put her glass on the table.

Slowly, she got to her feet and came around the table to where Jack was waiting for her. Jack took her hand and walked her to the far end of the floor, leaning over and whispering to her as soon as they were out of earshot, "I should have known. You still haven't told him about us, have you?"

"No, I haven't," she admitted.

"I didn't think so. Why not?"

"Because—"

"Because what? Are you worried that he won't forgive you?"

"No," she replied, although the possibility had crossed her mind more than once. Not that she could blame him, really. If the situation were reversed, would she be able to forgive and forget? She doubted it.

"Then why not?"

"It isn't important."

Jack laid a hand on Lisa's waist and drew her toward him. The heat from his hands soaked through the flimsy fabric of her dress and burned into her skin. Heat rose deep inside her, and she recognized the sparks of desire she felt whenever he touched her.

The music was soft, a melody she recognized and had always loved. With his arm around her, they drifted slowly, his eyes holding hers. "Our marriage isn't important?" he questioned.

"That's not what I meant. Of course the marriage was important, but it was so short-lived, and I believed it was behind me. And since we'll be divorced before long, I didn't see any reason to mention it to Carter until now. I am going to tell him tonight. Later. After we get home."

"So if I happened to mention..."

At the stricken look on Lisa's face, Jack squeezed her hand. "Lighten up. I'm kidding. Don't worry. I won't spill the beans. I promise."

Lisa heaved a sigh of relief. Jack had told her he would do whatever it took to prevent her marriage to Carter. How far was he prepared to go? Could she trust him to keep their secret until she could explain it to Carter?

She had no choice. She had to hope that he would.

The music stopped, but Jack didn't release her. She was powerless to move. As the next song began, he drew her closer. She felt the hard strength of his body pressing her to him, and the touch of his hand on her back felt like a branding iron burning through the fine fabric of her dress. She heard a heartbeat, but whether it was hers or Jack's, she didn't know. She knew the moment had come when she should draw back. But the music and the wine conspired to make her want to prolong the contact.

"Have I told you how fabulous you look tonight? I'm having trouble keeping my hands to myself."

The way he was looking at her... Her breath caught

in her throat as she recalled the way those hands had touched her during their marriage, and the way his lips had felt against hers.

Her face reddened. "As ravishing as Eleanor Randolph?" Lisa teased, determined to squelch the flames of desire flickering in her veins.

He grinned, and Lisa couldn't help but smile back at him, "If a compliment is all it takes to make her day..." He let the rest of the sentence die. "But you," he added, "do you have any idea what that dress is doing to me?" he whispered, his minty breath fanning her flaming cheeks. "If I was Carter, I wouldn't be spending the night schmoozing with fat bald guys."

"Oh?" she breathed. "What would you be doing?" As soon as the words left her mouth, she regretted them. She knew she shouldn't be encouraging him, but she couldn't stop herself from asking, even though she knew by the seductive tone of his voice what his answer would be.

"I'd be alone with you, slowly slipping the zipper of that dress down, raining kisses down your neck to the hollow in your throat, then lower to the—"

"Stop it!" Lisa gulped, her throat dry. Her insides churned, and she felt a stab of heat deep inside. "What makes you think that later tonight Carter won't be doing just that?" Lord, what devilish streak inside her had made her say that? She was surprised that her voice sounded normal when, inwardly, she her nerve endings tingled and every cell in her body was on fire, sensations she had thought dead long ago.

Jack laughed, a deep resonant sound. "Because, my

sweet wife, the phrase 'premarital sex' isn't in your vocabulary. Isn't that true?"

He knew her so well, even after all this time. She opened her mouth to deny it, to wipe that knowing smirk off his face. She was tempted, so tempted, to describe the most erotic love scene she'd ever read, substituting her name and Carter's for the hero and heroine. She wanted to see his face when she told him that she and Carter couldn't get enough of each other in bed. It would serve him right. But she couldn't.

"Now, relax and enjoy the music," he said, applying faint pressure in the small of her back and twirling her dramatically.

He was right. Nothing was going to happen here. In public. She took in a deep breath and let it out slowly, feeling the tension in her muscles fading as the moment passed and she gave herself to the rhythm of the music.

When the last strains of the song faded, Jack looked down into her face without releasing his hold on her. "I'll see you soon, sweetheart," he whispered, his face so close she could almost feel his lips on hers.

She nodded, unable to speak. Then suddenly, he let his arms fall and stepped back. "I'll take you back to your table."

He placed his hand on her elbow and slowly led her back across the ballroom.

"Where's Carter?" she asked his mother. "I didn't see him on the dance floor."

Almost as soon as the words left her mouth, Carter appeared at her side. "I'm terribly sorry, darling, but there's been an accident at Randolph Place. I have to go out there."

"What happened?"

"I don't know the details yet. Something about scaffolding falling."

Lisa jumped up and grabbed her purse. "I'll come with you."

"There's no point. There's nothing you can do. Ask Mother to find the chauffeur and have him take you home. If it isn't too late by the time I'm finished, I'll call and fill you in on the details."

"It doesn't matter what time it is. Please come over as soon as you can. I need to talk—"

"Then I'll see you later," he said, skimmed a kiss across her cheek, and turned and left.

I'd walk home before I'd ask your mother for anything, Lisa vowed silently to Carter's back, while at the same time calculating how much money she had with her to pay cab fare. She only had twenty dollars with her. Not nearly enough to get her home.

"I'd be happy to drive you home," Jack offered. His eyes twinkled merrily, and he smiled with an innocence Lisa recognized as phoney.

Heavens, after the things he'd said to her while they were dancing, she'd be a fool to accept his offer. But it was either that or ask Eleanor Randolph for help.

Lisa smiled grimly. "Thanks, Jack. I'd appreciate it."

"Excellent idea, Brennan." Devon got up and signalled for one of the waiters, who disappeared and reappeared moments later with Lisa's coat.

Almost before she knew it, she'd been whisked outside and into the car parked at the curb.

"Gonna invite me up for a cup of coffee?" Jack asked later when he drew the car drew to a stop outside Lisa's apartment building. He turned to her, resting his arm on the steering wheel. She could barely discern his features in the darkness inside the car, but she detected a hint of playfulness in his voice.

Through the shadows, Lisa studied the expression on his face. Did he really want coffee—or something more?

As if he could somehow read her thoughts, he spoke again. "One cup of coffee. That's all."

Lisa considered it for a moment, then realized how foolish it would be to invite him into her apartment. "Sorry Jack. I have a terrible headache. I'm going to have a long, hot bath, and then I'm going to bed."

He opened his mouth to speak, but she didn't give him the chance before she voiced the question she knew would be on his mind. "Alone."

* * *

Jack watched Lisa as she walked up the steps to the front door of her apartment building and went inside. He could see her through the glass as she made her way to the elevator. He waited until she'd disappeared into the elevator before he drove away.

So she's going to tell him tonight, he thought. By tomorrow, she'll be free. At least he hoped Randolph would break off their engagement and leave the door open for him.

But what if he didn't? What if he forgave her? Then he'd have to resort to more drastic measures. He had to come up with a plan to get her back. But what?

The clock had just chimed one o'clock when Lisa heard a knock at the door. After checking through the peephole that it was Carter, she opened the door.

Her resolve to speak to him about her marriage to Jack fizzled out as she watched him trudge into the apartment. His face was drawn, and the sharp planes of his face were pronounced with fatigue.

"Let me get you a drink," Lisa offered, taking his overcoat and hanging it in the closet. He nodded absently and slumped down in the easy chair beside the fireplace while Lisa went into the kitchen and took ice cubes out of the freezer and poured a generous shot of bourbon over it.

He smiled weakly at her when she brought the glass to him, took a large sip, then got up and crossed the room to the window facing out over the park.

A few flakes of snow drifted down to blanket the park. Somewhere a few blocks away, a siren wailed, while closer, tires squealed as a motorist rounded a curve in the road a little too quickly.

Carter's back was to her, and his hands were buried deep in the pockets on his pants. He stared out, and for the first time, Lisa noticed a hint of defeat in the slight slump of his shoulders. "Three men were on the scaffolding hanging the chandelier in the south ballroom," he said softly. "One of the ropes snapped."

Lisa gave a startled gasp. "How are they?"

"One of the men has been transferred to a trauma center in critical condition. The other two were hurt, but not as seriously."

Lisa crossed the room to where he stood. She reached out and put her arms around him, resting her cheek on his back. "I'm so sorry, Carter."

"It seems that since we turned the soil to begin construction, it's been one thing after another. I'm beginning to think that this whole project is jinxed."

Lisa's heart went out to him. She'd never seen him in this condition, almost like a whipped puppy. "It's only another couple of weeks and then everything will be fine. I just know it."

Carter turned and put his arms around her. "I hope so," he whispered in her ear. "I certainly hope so. The only thing that's keeping me sane right now is knowing that you're there beside me, that at least there's one thing in my life that's right. Now what was it you wanted to speak to me about?"

Lisa felt as if he'd dug a knife into her heart. How could she break the news to him that she, the one person he was counting on, had deceived him. How could she add to his problems?

She had to, though. She couldn't go on this way, keeping this secret to herself, knowing that at any given moment, he could find out. Jack wouldn't tell him. She was sure of that. But what about someone else? She couldn't guarantee that tomorrow or the day after that, one of the guests at the hotel wouldn't be an old friend from high school or a college friend of Jack's who would inadvertently let the truth out.

No, as much as her timing could have been better, she had to do it.

ELEVEN

Carter's face was unreadable while Lisa told her story. The only indication that he was even listening was the tightening of his jaw and the way his hands clenched around his glass.

Her eyes brimmed with tears. Tears of sadness, tears of regret for the pain she was causing Carter, tears of guilt. She didn't know what more she could say or do to show him how sorry she was.

She wanted desperately to hear him say that it didn't matter, that he loved her enough to forgive her. The silence in the room said it all.

Without a word, he got up and went into the kitchen to pour himself another drink. She heard the refrigerator door close and the clink of ice cubes. She waited, unsure whether she should follow him or wait.

She didn't have to wait long. Within moments, he returned, stopping in the doorway. "Is that everything you have to tell me?"

The bitterness in his voice stunned Lisa. She'd expected him to be hurt and angry, but he was a reasonable man. Surely he'd understand when she explained...

"Yes," she said softly through a choking sob.

"You don't have a couple of children you've conveniently forgotten to mention too, do you?"

"No, of course not. You can't know how sorry I am. There must be some way to make it up to you—"

Carter crossed the room and stood within inches. He gazed at her as if he'd never seen her before and took a sip of his drink. "You're sorry?" He laughed bitterly. "You're sorry. You've deceived me from the moment we met, led me to believe you'd never had sex with another man, and now you say you're sorry? You may be, but I don't think I can ever forgive you."

"Carter—"

"Please don't make this any worse than it is," he said, putting his empty glass on the table and turning towards her. "I can't marry someone I can't trust."

"I understand why you're angry—"

"You said you loved me," he interrupted. "Was that a lie too?"

"No," she insisted. "I do love you."

Carter shook his head as if he didn't believe her. "How can I believe anything you say after what you've done? What about Brennan? Do you still love him, too?"

Did she? Good question. Emotions flowed over her whenever she was with Jack and whenever she thought about him, but were those emotions love? She didn't know.

"My marriage to Jack was an important part of my life. I admit that. The feelings I have for Jack are simply memories of a magical summer when I thought life was perfect."

"I'm sorry Lisa. Perhaps in time I'll understand why you didn't tell me about this, but right now, I can't."

Tears rolled unchecked down Lisa's cheeks. Through the blur of tears, she slipped the diamond ring off her finger and held it out to Carter.

When he didn't take the ring from her outstretched hand, she glanced up at him. Why wasn't he taking it? Did he think there was still hope for them?

Carter paused for a moment, his gaze locked on the ring in her palm. Finally, he said, "How many others know about your marriage?"

"Only Karen," Lisa replied. When she'd moved to the city, she'd left the past behind, and had never mentioned her short-lived marriage to anyone. The only other person who knew was her sister, and after the divorce—or rather, what she'd thought was a divorce—she'd never mentioned Jack's name again, even though Lisa knew that Karen hadn't approved of the way she'd handled the whole situation.

In Karen's opinion, Lisa should have fought harder to save her marriage, and should have confronted Jack face-to-face. Looking back, maybe Karen had been right. At least if she had, these feelings wouldn't be bubbling to the surface now. She would have dealt with them then, and it would have been over for good. Closure, or something like that.

"I see."

"And Jack of course."

"Of course," he echoed, the sarcasm in his voice evident.

"Why?"

Carter lifted his head to look directly into her eyes. "I'd like to make one request," he said, wrapping his hand around hers and closing her fist over the ring. "Since the opening is only a few days away, I'd like you to consider keeping our breakup confidential until then."

Lisa's brows knitted together in frown. "I...suppose I could do that. But why?"

"Because," he explained, "under the circumstances, I'd like to avoid any more publicity than we've already had. What with the accident last night, and the implications that we're in financial difficulties, I'd like to avoid giving the press anything else to write about. Especially my personal life."

"Oh."

"Will you do that for me, at least until the grand opening and the ribbon-cutting ceremony? After it's over, we'll announce that the wedding is being postponed indefinitely. Gradually people will forget."

Lisa considered his request. After what she had done, it seemed like a small price to pay. She nodded in agreement and placed the ring back on her finger.

"Thank you," he muttered. "I truly wish I could understand why you didn't tell me the truth at the beginning, but I don't. Goodbye, Lisa." He turned, picked up his overcoat, and left.

As she stared at the closed door, the reality of the situation sinking in. She'd expected Carter to be upset and angry, but she'd believed that he cared enough for her to overlook her mistakes. But he hadn't.

Why didn't it hurt more? Sure, she'd cried a few tears, but shouldn't she feel as if her heart had been torn out? Memories of another time, when she'd learned that Jack didn't want her, surfaced. She remembered the pain, no, the absolute agony of knowing that the man she loved was turning his back on her. Shouldn't she feel that way now? Why didn't she?

She was hurt. She'd admit that. When she really analyzed it, though, it was only her pride that had taken a beating. In all honesty, she had a sense of relief, of suddenly being able to breathe freely, of having a weight taken off her shoulders.

Why?

She slumped into an overstuffed armchair while she pondered the answers to the questions that tumbled through her mind.

The knock at the door fifteen minutes later startled her. She padded to the door, each step accentuating the pounding in her head. With eyes that felt as though they were filled with sand, she pressed an eye against the peephole.

It was Jack.

Jack heard the click of the deadbolt turning, and for a second or two, he regretted the impulse that had led him to knock on Lisa's door. He had no business here. But he couldn't stay away. He had to know if she'd told Carter about them, and how he'd reacted to the news. At the same time, he was afraid to find out.

The second Lisa opened the door, Jack had his answer. One look at her tear-streaked face told him what he needed to know. Her eyes were puffy and red, and there was a trail of mascara running down both cheeks. She held a crumpled tissue in her hand.

She was still wearing that dress that skimmed over her curves, but now her feet were bare and her hair was a mass of dishevelled curls.

Jack recognized that part of him that wanted to tear Carter apart for the pain he'd caused Lisa. A bigger part of him couldn't help but be glad he'd broken up with her. Now, assuming that Lisa's tears weren't tears of joy, Jack might have a chance to win her back. As long as he didn't blow it again.Lisa opened the door wide to let him in. Was she angry? He couldn't tell by the blank expression on her face.

He slipped his jacket off and draped it on the back of a chair. "You look like he—"

"Thank you," she replied sarcastically.

Her perfume followed him as he slid past her into the living room.

"What are you doing here, Jack?" she asked. "I told you the coffee shop was closed."

"I was in the neighbourhood...just passing by..."

"Liar."

"Okay." He offered her a sheepish grin. "You caught me. You didn't look very well when I left you earlier. I came by to check on you. I saw your lights were still on..."

Lisa couldn't decide whether to be angry or touched. He'd gone out of his way to be a perfect gentleman all evening, other than the few racy comments he'd made while they were dancing. And those were as natural to Jack as breathing. In fact, she realized, she'd be more concerned if he didn't have anything suggestive to say. It just wasn't in his nature to be restrained. Whatever Jack had to say, he said it. He'd always been like that, and it was one of the things she'd loved about him. She could count on him to tell her the truth. He'd always been honest with her, even when that honesty had hurt her, or had made her angry.

But he shouldn't have come here. What if Carter had stayed just a few minutes longer? How would she have explained Jack's appearance at this time of night, especially now?

As if he could read her mind, he added, "I'm not a total idiot. I checked. The Porsche wasn't in the parking lot, so I figured it was safe to come up."

At least he'd had enough sense to do that.

"So, I'm guessing by the way you look that you told him," Jack said.

She nodded.

"And?"

She repeated the gist of the conversation she'd had with Carter, leaving out some of the nastier things he'd said to her. "I agreed to keep the break-up a secret until after the opening."

Jack raked his hand through his hair. "Why did you agree to that?"

"It seemed like a small request considering how much I'd hurt him. He has so much on his mind right now that if I can ease it even a little, I think it's the only decent thing to do. None of this is his fault."

Jack muttered something Lisa couldn't make out and stuffed his hands in his pockets, staring at her as if she had just landed from another planet.

"It's none of your business anyway," she pointed out. She glared at him, daring him to contradict her. He didn't.

"You're right," he muttered grimly, his lips pressed into a tight line.

She glanced up at him, the suspicion in her eyes evident. What was he up to? Jack never conceded a point without an argument, even when he knew he was wrong.

He let out a small laugh. "I know what you're thinking. You expect me to argue, but I've grown up a bit since those days when I'd argue just for the sake of it."

She couldn't help but laugh with him. He did know her so well. He'd always known what she was thinking, almost before she knew it herself.

"Are you okay?" he asked, concern creeping back into his voice.

Lisa shrugged. "I don't know. I'm angry that he doesn't love me enough to say it doesn't matter, and I'm hurt that even now, his first thought was for what the adverse publicity could do to the opening of the hotel. But at the same time, I'm relieved that it's over. I'll feel better in the morning. Right now it feels as if there's a band of steel drums playing a Latin rumba in my head."

"Well then, you're in luck. Didn't you know that I am the all-time headache-curing champion?"

Lisa's eyebrows arched.

"Why don't you go and change into something more comfortable—"

"Go home, Jack."

"And miss the opportunity to show off my doctoring skills? A little massage—"

"There will be no massage," Lisa put in. She couldn't help but chuckle, even though the slight motion of her head made the pounding in her head worse. "If you're trying to seduce me, I'm not impressed by your technique," she teased, starting to relax. Jack had always had that effect on her. "Can't you come up with a better line—?"

Jack closed the distance between them. He was so close she could feel his breath on her face. He raised his finger and lightly ran it down her cheek. Lisa felt as if he was forging a trail of fire on her skin. "Believe me," he whispered, "when I make love to you again, we won't need any worn-out lines to enhance the mood. Now scoot."

He gripped her shoulders, gently turned her away from him and gave her a gentle shove. She glanced over her shoulder to see him disappearing into the tiny kitchen, humming the melody of an old song she recognized from their high school days.

Lisa headed towards the bedroom, concentrating on moving her legs which had suddenly turned into jelly.

Quickly, she slipped into an oversized cotton T-shirt and a pair of sweat pants that had seen better days. She paused in front of the bedroom mirror and gave herself a satisfied glance. *That should do it. Only a blind man could be turned on by the way I look now.*

She slipped on a pair of furry slippers and padded softly back to the living room. Jack was still in the kitchen, so she curled up in a corner of the couch and closed her eyes, resting her head on a throw cushion. Her lips quirked in a soft smile as she listened to the sounds of him puttering in the kitchen. Pots and pans clattered, cupboard doors slammed, the tap ran. People have concocted gourmet meals with less noise, she mused. But she didn't really mind. The apartment seemed very empty and cold sometimes. Yet now, it seemed warm, cozy almost. And it seemed natural somehow for Jack to be here, in her apartment, doing - what was he was doing in there anyway?

"Here we are," Jack announced with a smile a few minutes later when he came out of the kitchen. He had a dish towel folded over his arm like a waiter in a five-star restaurant, and he was carrying a small silver tray holding two mugs and a plate of chocolate chip cookies. He brought the tray into the living room and set it down on the coffee table. "Dr. Jack's famous all-purpose healing remedy. Cures headaches, insomnia, arthritis...libido malfunctions," he added with a wink.

He picked up one of the mugs and handed it to Lisa. "Now drink up."

Lisa sniffed at the steaming brown liquid in the mug and caught a faint whiff of spice. "What is it?"

"Secret recipe. I'd tell you, but then I'd have to kill you," he said with a wicked grin.

Lisa grinned back. "Oh. Well, in that case ..." She lifted the mug to her lips and took a small sip. It was surprisingly good, tasting of chocolate and something else she couldn't put a finger on. Even the aroma itself seemed to immediately relax the tension in her muscles.

"I can't quite place the taste...but it does taste good. Is it cinnamon?"

Jack nodded. "That's all I'm telling you. But it is guaranteed to make you feel better in minutes," Jack promised, as he picked up the other mug and drank deeply from it.

"Are you having the same?" she asked.

"Uh-huh."

"So," Lisa asked, forming a serious expression, "which of the ailments you described are you trying to cure?"

A slow smile crept over his face. "I'll never tell."

While Lisa sipped at the mysterious 'headache remedy', Jack got up and switched off the overhead light, leaving the room bathed in only the soft light from a small table lamp in the corner.

"Uh, Jack, what do you think you're doing?" As if she needed to ask.

"I get the feeling you don't trust me," Jack protested

with a crooked grin, "but I assure you my motives are honorable. Your headache will go away faster without bright lights."

"Oh," Lisa replied sheepishly. She'd concede that point.

Jack paused in front of the collection of photographs on the fireplace mantle and picked up a silver frame holding a photo of Lisa's nephews taken at the beach the previous summer.

"Cute kids. Who are they?" he asked.

"Karen's twins. That's Kevin on the right. Tyler's the one in the baseball hat."

"How old are they?" Jack asked, his gaze still focused on the photograph. He seemed genuinely interested, and it took very little encouragement to get Lisa started on the adventures and misadventures of her younger sister's twins.

"They're almost six." She grinned, her eyes lighting up. "They'll be seven next month. I bought them each a battery-operated car that they can actually drive."

Jack looked at Lisa with interest. "A little extravagant, isn't it?"

Lisa shrugged. "Probably. But I don't care. Oh, you should see them, Jack. They're the most terrific kids. Normal, boisterous daredevil kids, but they are so bright, and so much fun..." Her voice trailed off.

Jack put the photograph back and crossed to Lisa. "So why are you loving someone else's kids when you should be loving your own?"

Lisa's throat went dry. *Because you were supposed to be the father of our children. And you were gone.* The words died on her lips. "I was trying to build a career—"

"Was it worth it?"

Lisa didn't respond. She couldn't, because she didn't know the answer. Her career was satisfying, from a professional point of view, but deep inside, far beneath the Brooks Brothers business suits and the cool efficient image she'd honed to perfection, was the woman who yearned to have a child of her own to hold in her arms.

"You've short-changed yourself, Lisa. You were made to be a mother to a whole brood of kids. You know that."

Yes, she knew that. She also knew that it was never going to happen. She and Carter had discussed the possibility of having a family, but Carter was quite content to be childless, and she had agreed. It had seemed like a small concession at the time, but the more she was with the twins, the harder it was to accept that little arms would never wind around her neck and call her 'mommy'. But, she realized, since Carter and she were finished, it was a moot point anyway.

"How could you give that up? That's all you ever talked about."

"Stop it, Jack, please." Her voice broke, the sudden realization of the sacrifice she'd made hitting her. She'd made the choice freely to remain childless, and she would live with it. If her sister's children were a substitute, then they were a wonderful substitute, and the love she showered on them certainly couldn't hurt them. "You'd better go," she mumbled softly.

"I'm sorry. I had no right to say that." In less than a heartbeat, Jack was on the sofa beside her.

Hot tears pricked her eyelids and she had an over-whelming urge to throw herself into his arms and sob her eyes out. It must be the headache that was making her react like that, she reasoned. Either that, or it was a side effect of Jack's 'headache remedy'. What had he put in that drink, anyway?

"Here," Jack said, taking her hand. "Lie down and close your eyes for a few minutes. I guarantee your headache will disappear."

Lisa's senses were on red alert before he'd even moved to pull a soft throw from the back of the sofa. "Not a chance, Jack," she retorted. "You don't think I'm stupid enough to fall for that old trick, do you?"

The frustrated expression in Jack's eyes was echoed in his voice when he spoke. "You think I'm stupid enough to use that old trick to seduce you? I outgrew that one when I was in high school."

A crooked grin crossed Lisa's face. "I guess not."

"Good. Now do what you're told." Jack grabbed a pillow and put it at the end of the couch, punching it a couple of times to fluff it up.

Fatigued washed over Lisa, and she lifted her feet up and settled her head into the cushion, sighing tiredly as Jack tucked the throw around her.

"Now close your eyes."

"You should go."

"As soon as you're asleep, I'll let myself out," he promised.

Lisa closed her eyes, already feeling the fuzzy-warm sensation of sleep creeping up on her. A warmth stole over her, and she couldn't force her eyes open.

She heard Jack pick up the empty cups and take them into the kitchen, washing them out and setting them back on the cup hooks under the cabinet. Doing anything quietly was beyond him, she thought, unable to prevent the faint smile she knew was showing on her face.

TWELVE

Lisa's even breathing when he went back into the living room convinced Jack that she was sound asleep. Her face was flushed and a slight smile played on her lips. He couldn't remember ever feeling more protective, as if he wanted to keep her that close to him forever.

He perched himself on the edge of the coffee table at her side. Just looking at her filled him with such a fierce tightness in his chest he couldn't stand to not touch her.

Tenderly, he reached over the brushed a strand of hair from her cheek and touched his lips to her forehead. *How can I convince her that I was wrong? How do I make her see that she belongs with me?*

Shaking his head as the unanswered questions filled his brain, he got up and crossed the room. "I will find a way," he promised aloud, giving Lisa a loving glance and picking up his overcoat. "Believe me, I will", he repeated as he grabbed his jacket and let himself out of the apartment.

Both the headache and Jack were gone when Lisa woke up. Sunshine spilled through the curtains she hadn't bothered to close the night before, and already the air conditioning was running full blast.

The room seemed cold, yet Lisa knew that it wasn't the air temperature that was chilling her, but that she was alone, alone with only the faint scent of Jack's spicy aftershave as a reminder that he had been here.

She'd never felt this way before, and she shivered involuntarily. What is he doing to me? she asked the empty room as she drew the throw more tightly around her shoulders. Questions tumbled through her mind. Why couldn't he leave her alone to get on with her life? Even though her engagement to Carter was over, he couldn't really believe she'd take the chance on him breaking her heart again, could he? And if he really did want her back, why hadn't he told Carter about their marriage himself instead of waiting for her to break the news to him? No, she decided finally, he's annoyed because for once, he can't have what he wants.

But what did she want? Lately, she didn't know. She'd been so sure that marrying Carter would make her happy, yet now, whenever Jack was with her, she felt a sense of contentment missing the rest of the time. And now that Jack was gone, he'd left behind a void that she couldn't fill.

A sigh rippled through her, and she closed her eyes, willing herself to go back to sleep.

Annie, Lisa's executive assistant, plucked the file folder from the out tray on the corner of the desk the next Friday morning and handed it to her with a frustrated grin. "Finally," she muttered. "Honestly, those jokers downstairs don't know their a—" She stopped in mid-sentence and offered Lisa a grin. "Well, they don't."

Lisa chuckled. It wasn't difficult to fill in the rest of the sentence for herself. "Thanks," she said. "This is exactly what I've been waiting for. I was wondering how long they would take to put these stats together."

She opened the folder, her gaze skimming over the columns of figures on the computer printout.

"By the way, there's a bunch of flowers on your desk," Annie said, handing Lisa a mug of coffee from the coffeemaker on the credenza behind her desk. "Is Carter in the doghouse?"

Carter? Why would he be in trouble? If anything, it was she who should be sending flowers. The thought that perhaps Carter had forgiven her after all warmed her inside. She hadn't seen Jack all week, and even though it had given her time to think, she had to admit she missed him. Every time the phone rang or someone came to the door, she'd expected it to be him.

And ever since Carter had left her apartment the previous Saturday night, she'd felt that he was avoiding her. Any contact between them had come through email or messages from assistant to assistant. It seemed nobody had noticed, though, and for that she was thankful.

Annie motioned with her head to Lisa's office. "Take a look," she said. "They came about fifteen minutes ago."

With a smile, Lisa crossed the carpeted outer office, Annie following close behind. As soon as she opened the door to her office, the heady perfume of the flowers overwhelmed her senses. It filled the room, and the memory of that very fragrance hit her as suddenly as if she had been physically stricken.

There, arranged in a crystal vase on the corner of her desk, was a huge bouquet of honeysuckle blooms. Lisa didn't have to read the card tucked inside the blooms to know that the flowers weren't from Carter. They were from Jack.

She dropped her purse and briefcase on the chair beside the desk and leaned over to inhale the sweet perfume.

"I must admit I was surprised when the delivery boy brought them. I figured him more for a roses kind of guy, not honeysuckle. I didn't even think honeysuckle was available at this time of year."

"They're perfect," Lisa murmured, suddenly feeling happier than she had all week. A memory surfaced, and she smiled to herself, recalling a time long ago when Jack had arrived at her door with a huge bouquet of honeysuckle. She'd asked him where he'd picked them and he'd confessed to raiding the honeysuckle vine covering the trellis beside her house. When she asked him why he'd done that, he'd replied simply, 'because I love you'.

He'd remembered. The thought brought a soft smile to her lips. She reached in and extricated the small card from the blooms, recognizing the scrawl on the front of the envelope. Her fingers trembled as she opened the envelope, her face warming as she read the message. "To bring you sweet dreams," the card said. A chuckle escaped her when she read the signature. "Dr. Cure-all", it read.

"You're blushing," Annie pointed out, craning her neck to get a look at the handwriting on the card.

Flustered, Lisa shoved the card into her jacket pocket and turned away. "Don't be silly. I am not."

Annie laughed. "Yes you are. You're blushing like a schoolgirl who's just received a note from the boy she's got a mad crush on."

Like the schoolgirl she'd been the first time Jack brought her flowers.

Taking a deep breath to calm the fluttering in her heart, she turned to Annie. "Is Carter in?" she asked, trying desperately to change the subject.

"Uh-huh," Ann replied, "but if I were you, I'd run for cover. I don't know what the man's problem is, but he's like a lion with a thorn in his paw this morning."

"Thanks," Lisa said, then slid into the chair at her desk and opened the file folder to study the computer printout more closely. Annie left and closed the door behind her.

Before she had a chance to make any sense out of

the numbers, she heard Carter's voice a split second before Annie opened her door.

"Carter just called," Annie said. "He wants to see you in his office pronto. He sounds pretty mad."

Lisa glanced up from the papers in her hand, surprise registering on her face. Annie gave her a sympathetic glance, then shrugged and rolled her eyes.

"He's been that way all morning," Annie added before she went back to her own desk.

Terrific, Lisa thought, dropping the papers back on her desk. He's going to be really annoyed when he hears that the linen supply company has threatened to refuse credit until their outstanding bills are paid.

Her knees threatened to buckle as she crossed the outer office and went into Carter's office. What's the matter with you? she chided herself. There's no reason for nerves. The worst is over.

Carter was standing with his back to her, but even from a distance, she could see the tension in the set of his shoulders. He had several file folders in his hand, and he was arranging them in his briefcase. A small flight bag sat on the floor near his feet.

"Is something wrong, Carter?"

"I'm flying back to New York this afternoon," he said brusquely, a strange expression that Lisa didn't recognize crossing his face. For a fleeting moment, Lisa wondered if he was uncomfortable being alone with her under the circumstances. No, she decided, Carter was much too self-confident to feel awkward. It must have been her imagination.

"Again?" she asked. "Why?"

There it was again, that same expression, disappearing in a split second. "Nothing you need to concern yourself with. I'm only telling you in case there are any emergencies while I'm gone. You are in charge when I'm away, remember?"

"Of course I remember," Lisa snapped back. She wasn't sure why he'd evaded her question, since she was the assistant manager. At the same time a sense of relief that washed over her. At least she wouldn't have to deal with him on a day-to-day basis. Perhaps by the time he returned, she'd have had more time to come to grips with the fact that her future with Carter was over.

In two long strides, he stood directly in front of her, so close she could see the tiny scar above his lip that he'd received when he'd fallen off his bicycle when he was a child.

"Do you think you can handle the final preparations for the opening by yourself, or should I call my mother and have her give you some assistance?"

Lisa felt herself bristle. Even the mere suggestion that she wasn't capable of finishing the job irritated her, and she was tempted to point out in no uncertain terms that it was she who'd organized the entire event - without any help from him *or* his mother. Instead, she plastered a smile on her face that she hoped would hide her anger. "Don't worry, Carter. Everything's under control." She sat down on the edge of the chair in front of his desk. "The invitations went out almost a month ago. The mayor has already confirmed, and two of the members of the city council will be here. I've prepared press releases for all the major newspapers and media, and I've assured the photographers that we'll be happy to give them all the photo opportunities they could ask for. I've also arranged to give Southern Hotels Monthly a behind-the-scenes look at the new building and an exclusive interview."

"Good. That's good." It was obvious he was distracted. "Well, if you need help—"

"I'll call on your mother if I need her." When pigs fly, she added to herself.

"And you'll honor our...arrangement."

Try as she might, Lisa couldn't keep a tinge of bitterness out of her voice when she answered. "I said I'd continue the charade. I don't go back on my word."

Carter opened his mouth to speak, and looked as if he might contradict her statement, then obviously changed his mind. "Fine," he muttered, picking up his briefcase and heading toward the door. "I'll see you at the ribbon-cutting."

Without even a civil goodbye, he stalked out. Lisa stood in the center of his office and watched him disappear into the elevator on the other side of the reception area.

Lisa yawned as she glanced at her watch. It was just after noon, and already she was exhausted. She'd been at the hotel since before dawn, checking and double-checking the arrangements for the ribbon-cutting, greeting guests and giving interviews to the media that had descended on the hotel lobby before eight a.m.

Everything had been perfect. The official ribbon-cutting had gone off without a hitch, lunch was delicious, and the invited guests were impressed with the hotel and the service it promised. The best part was yet to come though. Even though she felt as if she could sleep for a week, the excitement stirring in the pit of her stomach made it difficult to sit still for a second.

Carter got up and climbed the three steps to the small stage at the far end of the ballroom. One of the staff handed him a microphone.

This was it! What she had worked for since the day she'd come to work for the Randolph organization right out of college.

"Thank you all for coming," Carter began, then paused while the voices faded into silence in the main dining room of Randolph Place. His eyes scanned the room, and he smiled with satisfaction.

"This is a very special day," he went on. "Now that Randolph Place has officially opened, I will be acting as general manager of this hotel, and I'll be handing over the reins at Randolph Plaza to a worthy successor who has proved beyond a doubt to be more than capable to fill the position I will be leaving vacant."

Lisa sat perched on the edge of her seat. Her heart thundered in anticipation and excitement. Her fingers trembled and she said a silent prayer that her legs wouldn't buckle when Carter introduced her and she had to walk from her seat near the end of the head table to take the microphone from him.

She could feel the eyes of everyone in the room resting on her, and for a moment, she had the urge to check that all the buttons on her jacket were fastened, she had no runs in her hose, or that her slip wasn't hanging down below her plum-colored wool skirt.

Instead, she took a few deep breaths and smiled confidently at Carter. No matter what happened in Carter's personal life, he never let it interfere with business. Now, even after everything that had happened between them, she was sure he wouldn't let their personal problems come between them in their working relationship. And surely, once he'd thought about it, he would come to understand why she had deceived him, and he would forgive her.

Carter's voice filtered into her thoughts. "And now, without further ado, I'd like to introduce the new manager of Randolph Plaza." He turned and smiled in her direction. Lisa smiled back, and for some inexplicable reason, she suddenly felt sure that things would work out.

Lisa put her napkin on her plate and started to rise, running a hand down her skirt to smooth any imaginary wrinkles.

"Brian Palmer."

The smile froze on her face, and the words echoed in her ears. Brian Palmer. The night manager from the Randolph Plaza in New York. This couldn't be happening. Carter wouldn't do this to her.

As she slumped back into her seat, she heard the

applause fill the room, and the man seated beside her rise and make his way to the podium. Her glance followed him as he shook Carter's hand and took his place at the microphone.

He began to speak, but Lisa didn't hear the words. Her eyes were fixed on Carter, who looked directly at her and smiled, then turned away. Had anyone else noticed how his eyes held revenge, and how his lips curled into a sneer? Or was it her imagination?

From where he was sitting at a round table near the podium, Jack watched the silent exchange between Lisa and Carter. Fiery rage coursed through him, and it took every ounce of self-control he had to stay in his seat when all he wanted to do was erase that self-satisfied smirk from Randolph's face.

He had to admit Lisa was handling the shock well, though. Like the professional she was, she smiled, applauded, and appeared to be totally in control. Jack knew better. He'd known Lisa long enough to know exactly what was going on behind that calm facade.

Palmer finished his address and returned to his seat, and shortly after, the guests began to mingle. Jack spoke to several acquaintances, and by the time he reached the head table, Lisa was gone. He glanced around the room, searching for her. There was no sign of her, but he did see Carter sipping a glass of champagne with several guests near the doors leading to lounge area holding several sofas and tables.

Eyes locked on the man smiling affably at something being said to him, Jack crossed the room, his heart pumping, the adrenaline coursing through his body. He stopped directly in front of Carter. "You sonofabitch." Jack balled his hands into fists and jammed them into his pockets. That was the only thing that would prevent him from beating Carter to a pulp right here.

The guests nearby quieted. Carter glanced towards him, then turned to his companion, a woman Jack recognized as the publisher of one of Miami's leading magazines. "Excuse me a moment. It seems Mr. Brennan is upset about something."

"Looking for your wife?" Carter hissed when he and Jack moved away. "She's being escorted out of the building as we speak."

"Of all the dirty tricks—"

"Look, Brennan. It's strictly business," Carter retorted. "Now that I can't keep an eye on her, I can't have her in a position of power, can I? There's no way of knowing what kind of trouble she could cause, now that I've dumped her."

"She deserved that job—"

"That's irrelevant."

"You used her—"

"Not as much as I should have apparently."

Jack's eyebrows raised. "What's that supposed to mean?"

"She led me to believe she was pure and that she was saving herself for our marriage."

"So?"

"How pure could she be when she'd already been married? What was she like in your bed, Brennan? What else didn't I know about her? I'll bet she was a little tiger—"

Before he could help himself, Jack raised his fist and planted it square in Carter's face. Carter reeled from the blow. Blood spurted from his nose and dripped on his white shirt. His eyes bulged, and as he dug into his trouser pocket for a tissue, he sputtered, "I'll have you charged for this, Brennan."

Jack grinned. "Go ahead, Randolph. It was worth it. Just remember that the press will have a field day when they find out why I slugged you." He picked up a napkin from the table and offered it to Carter. "Here. You're gonna need it."

Jack turned away. He couldn't help smiling as he rubbed his fist with his other hand while he crossed the room. He swore. That had hurt!

THIRTEEN

"This is getting to be a habit," Lisa said later that night when she arrived home to find Jack sitting in the corridor outside her door. She hadn't been able to face her empty apartment after she'd left the hotel so she'd driven around, finding herself at the beach where she'd sat and watched the surf until the clouds rolled in and it started to rain.

Jack had a brown paper bag in his hand, and as she approached, he produced a bottle of her favorite wine.

"You're late," he commented as she unlocked the door and stepped inside. "Where have you been? I've been waiting for ages."

"None of your business," she replied caustically.

"You okay?"

Lisa glanced up at Jack. He seemed genuinely concerned. She didn't want him to care. She didn't want his pity. She wanted to be left alone to nurse her wounds. Something in his eyes forced her to tell the truth. "No, I'm not. I never expected it. He blindsided me—"

Jack reached for her, and she slid into the waiting circle of his arms. The fresh scent of him filled her nostrils, and the roughness of the fabric of his jacket grazed her cheek. She could hear the pounding of his heart, and his arms around her gave her such a feeling of safety and security that the tears began to fall.

He held her in silence until her sobs ceased. Finally, she pulled away and ran her hand over his jacket. She gave him a weak smile. "Sorry," she said softly, "I got you wet. I seem to be doing a lot of crying lately. I don't know what's wrong with me. I never cry."

"You can cry on my shoulder any time," he whispered. "Would it make you feel better to know that it's unlikely Carter will be appearing in public for a few days?"

Lisa's brows narrowed in a frown. "Why? What did you do?"

Jack told her, omitting some of the details of their conversation.

"You shouldn't have done that," she said sternly when he'd finished.

Jack grinned. "I know. But it felt so good."

Lisa chuckled in spite of herself. "What if he calls the police?"

"Trust me. He won't."

Suddenly, thunder boomed outside and the lights flickered. "It's getting nasty outside. You'd better go," Lisa murmured. "We're in for a storm."

Jack ignored her. "Did you get the flowers?" he asked.

"Yes, I did. Thank you. They're beautiful," she said grudgingly. "But that was a dumb thing to do, sending them to the office. Everyone thought they came from Carter. I guess it doesn't matter what anyone thinks now, does it?" she said with a wry grin.

Jack shrugged and smiled, revealing the dimple in his cheek. "Did you tell them who they were really from?"

"No, I didn't. Why did you send them?"

"Their petals reminded me of your lips. Soft and—"

"Jack. Stop it." Lisa felt the heat rise in her cheeks at his blatant admiration. His words were pure blarney, as her grandmother would say, but nevertheless, it gave her little goosebumps to hear Jack's low sexy voice uttering the words.

If she wasn't careful, she'd fall under the same spell he'd cast on her so many years ago with his flattery. She couldn't afford to let her guard down. "Why did you come here, Jack? Especially on a night like this."

"I didn't think you should be alone, so I thought I'd drop by and keep you company."

"I don't need company."

Jack's eyebrows raised. "I do."

"Then get a dog." Lisa kicked off her shoes and dropped her purse on the chair, then headed into the kitchen. Jack followed behind.

"Ooh! Such hostility. If I thought you were giving me a hint, I might be hurt."

Lisa couldn't help but laugh. Nothing short of a sledgehammer to the head would give Jack a hint.

"Where do you keep your wine glasses?" he asked, opening every cupboard door in the small kitchen.

"Here," she said, reaching into the cabinet directly above her head and taking out one glass.

"One glass?"

"I don't want wine."

"You know it isn't healthy to drink alone," he said. "Have a small one with me."

Fine," she acquiesced. "But make it a small one, and then go home. I'm not in the mood to entertain."

Jack held up his hands in mock surrender. "Fair enough," he agreed, reaching over her head to get another glass. Lisa caught a whiff of his aftershave, and a few strands of his hair brushed her cheek as he leaned against her.

Lisa got up and put her glass on the counter several minutes later, then moved towards the door. She had to get rid of him. He was far too desirable, far too close.

Suddenly, Jack's arms closed around her, pulling her gently toward him.

"Jack, please..." She lifted her hand and resting it against his chest to stop him.

Lisa felt his arms tighten around her, his hands sweeping with aching longing over her body, his breath fanning her cheek. How could she have thought, even for an instant, that she could resist him. He'd been her first love, her only true love. She'd belonged to him heart and soul from the first moment she'd set eyes on him on the high school football field. And she still belonged to him.

She should have pulled away from him, knowing how it would end if she didn't. But she couldn't.

Then his mouth captured hers. She parted her lips willingly when he demanded the intimacy. A sigh escaped from her throat.

She'd been telling herself ever since Jack had appeared in the hotel lobby that what they had together was gone, that what she had felt for him was dead and could never be resurrected.

But she'd been wrong. Oh, how wrong she'd been. The sensations were still there, stronger than ever, melting away all the years they'd been apart.

Jack drew his mouth away. "You still love me, don't you?" It was a statement rather than a question.

"I...Jack...we have to stop..."

"Why?" His voice was gruff, sexy. "We're still married."

His lips moved down her neck to kiss the line of her collar bone and his question—the million-dollar question—tumbled through her mind. Did she still love him?

There was no doubt in her mind. She did.

* * *

Weak sunshine was peeking through the clouds when Lisa woke. She glanced over at the alarm clock. Nine-twenty. Heavens, she hadn't slept that late in years.

"Hungry?" Jack asked from where he was standing

at the doorway to her bedroom. The night before, the storm had intensified and she'd told him he could spend the night, but not in her bed. He'd let out a sigh of resignation but he'd been smiling at the same time, so she'd given him blankets and pillows and left him to make himself comfortable on the sofa.

"Famished," Lisa replied. "Bacon and eggs or pancakes?"

"You have to ask?"

She laughed. She didn't. He'd always choose pancakes, especially with the blueberry syrup he'd introduced her to and that she always had in the refrigerator now.

"Mind if I grab a quick shower and then I'll help you?" he asked, not waiting for a reply before he headed into the bathroom.

The bathroom door closed before she had a chance to answer.

Her mind in a whirl, Lisa threw on the t-shirt and shuffled to the front door to retrieve the morning newspaper. Then, she went into the kitchen. Automatically, she put coffee in the filter and poured cold water into the reservoir. As the hot brown liquid began to fill the pot, she planned exactly what she would say to Jack as soon as he came out of the bathroom.

She was just taking two mugs out of the cupboard when she heard the bathroom door open. She poured the coffee and took the mugs to the kitchen table.

Jack appeared in the living room, a white bath towel draped around his waist. Lisa's heart thumped at the sight of his bare chest. "Do you have—?"

Suddenly, the front door burst open and two red-headed little boys bounded into the apartment, followed by a frazzled-looking young woman lugging a huge canvas bag.

"Karen!"

The boys raced over to Lisa and threw their arms around her bare legs. Feeling the cold hands on her bare skin reminded her that she had nothing on underneath the flimsy T-shirt.

Meanwhile, Karen had stopped in her tracks at the sight of Jack standing half-naked in the middle of the apartment. Her eyes would have been sitting on her cheekbones if they could, and her mouth hung open. Finally, she looked away and glanced over at Lisa, then immediately threw her glance back on Jack.

"Jack?" she whispered, as if she was seeing a ghost from the past. "Is that you?"

"In the flesh." Jack's face split into a grin.

Karen let out a groan at the corny pun.

"Sorry." He gave her a sheepish grin. "I couldn't resist. How are you, Karen?" Jack asked. "It's been a long time."

Honestly, Lisa thought, incensed. Jack actually seemed to be enjoying the reaction. That figured, somehow. Nothing ever seemed to faze him. Roll with the punches, he always used to say.

Heavens, she had to take control of the situation before it got completely out of hand.

"Who are you?" Tyler asked, gazing up at Jack with huge blue eyes.

"My name's Jack. I'm a friend of your aunt's."

"I'm Tyler. And that's Kevin."

Jack crouched down to get on an eye-to-eye level with the six-year-old. "How do you do," Jack said seriously, holding out his hand to Tyler.

Kevin appeared at Tyler's side and put out his hand as well. "Are you coming to the water park with us?" Kevin asked.

Jack glanced at Lisa, the question in his eyes. Lisa glared at him, telling him in no uncertain terms that he wasn't invited.

"You bet I am," he said. "I wouldn't miss it. But right now, how about we check out the cartoons on TV while your mom and aunt have a chat." He winked at Lisa, gave Karen a brilliant smile and disappeared into the bedroom hand-in-hand with the twins. Lisa heard the door click shut, and seconds later, the sounds of Elmer Fudd filled the room.

So he wasn't totally insensitive to the reaction he'd caused. He knew Karen must have a thousand questions, so he was going to occupy the twins so that she and Karen could talk uninterrupted. For that she was grateful.

"What's he doing here?" Karen gasped, her eyes huge. "And looking mighty good, I might add. Of course he always was a gorgeous hunk."

Yes, Lisa had to agree, he did look mighty good. And she had always thought he was as close to perfect physically as it was possible to be. And to top it off, he felt pretty darned good too. She felt her cheeks tingle at the memory of exactly how good he felt.

"Karen! What are you doing ogling other men? You're a married woman."

"Hmm," Karen murmured. "And so were you, until you let him get away."

"The divorce wasn't my idea, if you remember correctly."

"You could have contested it. You could have fought to save it. There's no way I would've let him get away. He would've had to pry me loose with a crowbar."

Yes, Lisa thought, she supposed she could have tried harder to save her marriage. But at the time, her self-confidence was at an all-time low, and her parents managed to convince her that it would be best if she let him go quietly.

"It doesn't matter now." For a few moments, Lisa considered telling her sister that she was legally still married to Jack. But almost as quickly, she decided against it. Karen wasn't fond of Carter, and had always had a soft spot in her heart for Jack, so she knew exactly what Karen would say. Things that she wasn't ready to hear right now.

"So what's going on? And why didn't you call me?"

"I've been busy—"

A wicked smile crossed Karen's face. "So I see."

"It isn't like that," Lisa protested. "Jack...well...it's a long story—"

"Aunt Lisa?" Kevin shouted from the bedroom. "Can we go soon?"

Lisa grinned, grateful for the reprieve, even though she was well aware her sister was like a bloodhound when she was digging for gossip. "How about some breakfast first and then we'll go? I'm making pancakes."

"They've already had breakfast but you know they'll eat anytime, anywhere," Karen said with a chuckle. Then she turned to her boys. "Come and give me a kiss goodbye."

When the hugs and kisses were taken care of, Karen moved toward the door while the boys retreated back to the bedroom. Karen made sure they were out of earshot when she whispered to Lisa, "And you'd better call me and tell me everything."

Lisa nodded. "I will. I promise."

By the time Lisa, Jack and the twins reached the water park, it was filled with people taking advantage of the sun after the storm the night before.

The sky was cloudless, and the sun was warm on their faces as Lisa unpacked hats and covered the twins with sunscreen.

She was annoyed, yet at the same time she was glad Jack was sharing the day with them. Then guilt set in, because she shouldn't want that.

The day passed in a pleasant blur. Lisa hadn't been to a water park in years, and with Jack and the twins, she relaxed and enjoyed playing in the sprinklers with them and sliding down the water slide. Jack fit right in with the boys, enjoying himself, too.

She should have known he would. He'd always been

a water-lover, and she couldn't help wondering if he still swam and surfed.

He'd tried to teach her to surf once, but after she'd fallen in for what seemed like the hundredth time, she'd given up. She'd been happy to watch him surf from the safety of the beach.

They were lucky to find a picnic table in a shaded area of the park, and after a lunch of sandwiches and fruit that Lisa had packed, she handed Kevin her phone with the timer set for a half hour. "When the timer goes off, we'll play some more."

She had to admit she hadn't enjoyed herself this much in a long, long time, and she realized just how much she missed the exercise. She'd been spending far too much time cooped up in her office lately, and she made herself a promise that she would get out more.

With the boys occupied with a hand-held video games they'd dug out of their bags, Lisa and Jack cleared away the trash from their lunch and chatted casually until the alarm on her phone rang.

Video games forgotten, Jack took the boys back to the small water slide.

"Look at me!" Tyler shouted from the top a minute later before he disappeared into the tube. Kevin was next, and Jack followed behind.

He made a huge splash when he hit the water. The twins raced over, their hoots of laughter ringing in the air. "Way to go, Jack," Kevin announced in a tone that said 'you're my hero'.

Jack grinned up at the two little boys. "Don't you

think Auntie Lisa needs to get wet, too?" he asked in his best villain voice.

The boys dissolved into gales of laughter. "Yeah!"

Lisa glared at him. He wouldn't dare, she thought. The thought entered her mind just as she felt her body being hoisted into the air and tossed into the water.

She came up sputtering. By this time, the twins' hysterical laughter filled the air, and even through her water-spiked lashes, she could see that they were having a wonderful time.

"You'll be sorry," she sputtered at Jack. "I'll get you for this."

She looked around, taking notice that what she had in mind wouldn't bother anyone else. No one was close to them in the pool, so before Jack had time to notice what Lisa was up to, she sent a wave of water into him.

That was all the incentive they needed. Before long, water was flying faster and thicker than the worst rainstorm they'd ever seen and their giggles could be heard on the next block.

At one point, Lisa leaned her back against the side of the pool, watching Jack with the twins. They'd warmed to him as if they'd known him forever, and if she didn't know better, she could have sworn he'd been raised with a whole houseful of siblings.

A bittersweet sensation filled her, and she felt her eyes fill with misty tears. She would never have children of her own. There would be no water fights, no picnics at the beach, no sailboat rides.

She'd made the choice. And until Jack's sudden appearance, she'd been convinced it was the right one.

FOURTEEN

It was dark by the time they got home. After their excursion, they'd walked up to the mall, where Jack had bought both boys a small toy. Then they'd eaten hamburgers and French fries at one of the local fast food places. On the way home in the car, Tyler had dozed off, but he woke up as Jack carried him upstairs to the apartment. While Lisa filled the kettle with water and put it on to boil, Jack took the boys into the bedroom and helped them to get ready for bed.

"Jack," Kevin said as Jack tucked the comforter under his chin. "Will you go to the water park with us again?"

"I will if your Aunt Lisa asks me to," Jack replied. He got up and crossed the room to the other bed, where Tyler was sitting cross-legged on top of the comforter. He pulled the covers down, and held them while Tyler slid inside, then covered him.

"That's okay," Kevin said. "She doesn't have to ask you. We will, and she doesn't never say no to us, does she, Ty?"

"Nope," Tyler agreed. "She always gives us anything we want. But we have to say please and thank you," he added, his voice growing serious. "We have to be polite."

Jack tried to hide the smile threatening to erupt. How well these two little boys knew their aunt.

"Jack?" Kevin's voice came again from the other side of the room.

"What is it, Kev?"

"Are you gonna marry Auntie Lisa?"

Jack gazed down at the little boy and smiled softly. "I sure hope so."

Kevin snuggled deeper beneath the blankets. "That's good," he murmured sleepily, then closed his eyes and rolled over onto his side away from Jack.

Jack sat down on the side of the bed for a few moments, wondering how even a six-year-old could see that Lisa and he were meant to be together, and the grown woman in the kitchen was fighting it so hard.

"We like you better than the other man," Tyler put in from the other bed. "Is that rude?"

"Not at all," Jack assured him, tousling his hair. "I really like you guys, too. Now sleep tight."

"Will you be here in the morning?"

Good question. If he had anything to say about it, he'd be here for the rest of his life. But he couldn't tell them that. "I hope so," he said instead, then switched off the small bedside lamp and closed the door.

"Are they asleep?" Lisa asked when he came back into the kitchen. She was folding a dish towel and hanging it over the oven door.

"Just about," Jack said, turning her around to face him. He placed one arm on each side, pinning her between him and the stove. His lips grazed hers. "Tyler asked me if I'll still be here in the morning."

He felt Lisa stiffen in his arms. "We have to talk," she said.

"Later," he whispered against her lips as he took her in a deep, passionate kiss.

Even though Lisa's brain protested, her body betrayed her. Jack's lips grazed hers, and the warmth deep inside began to seep through her once more. She melted against him as he kissed her. Lordy, how that man could kiss! She shouldn't be surprised, because he'd always been able to turn her insides to mush. The sound of a door closing shattered the mood. Lisa stiffened in Jack's arms, and pulled away. "Stop!"

Jack drew back, his breath ragged, his eyes glazed. "What? What's the matter?"

"I heard something. One of the boys must be up. I have to go check."

Lisa lifted her hands to Jack's chest, feeling his heartbeat pound beneath his t-shirt. She pushed against him. "Jack," she persisted. "Let me go. Right now."

"If you promise to come right back," he murmured,

his lips grazing her earlobe. Then he released her and stepped back, resting his back against the counter. "Remind me to explain to those kids about their lack of timing, will you?" he grumbled, but the lop-sided grin on his face told Lisa he wasn't really angry.

Lisa took a few deep breaths and straightened her blouse, then turned and left the kitchen. The bedroom door was closed, and she slowly turned the knob and opened it, slipping inside and tiptoeing to each of the twin beds.

Tyler's arm was wrapped tightly around the lamb she'd given him when he was born, and she gazed lovingly down at his sleeping face. A smile tugged at her lips.

Kevin had kicked off the blankets, and his hands were curled into tiny fists. He'd kicked off the thin blanket, so she covered him, and reached down to brush a stray lock of hair off his face.

Moonlight streamed through the windows, giving the boys an angelic look. Lisa couldn't take her eyes off them. They were so precious to her, she couldn't imagine feeling more love for a child of her own than she did for them. Yet she knew that she would.

But she would never have a child of her own.

This can't happen, she scolded herself. Not again. And the sooner Jack left, the easier it would be to get back in control of her emotions.

"Where were we?" Jack murmured, closing the gap between them as she came out of the spare room. Her bedroom door was open behind her, and Lisa was well aware why he had met her at this spot.

"Jack," Lisa began, "I think you should leave."

Jack's eyes flew open in surprise. "What?"

"Please go."

A frown crossed his forehead. "I thought that's what you said, but I figured I was hearing things."

Lisa's fingers were trembling. Every ounce of her being wanted to drag him into that bedroom and never leave, but reason and common sense told her that would be the biggest mistake of her life. Instead, she turned and closed the bedroom door, then stared directly into Jack's eyes to make sure he got the message.

"What's going on?"

"This is wrong."

"What's wrong?"

"This. Us. Us together."

"This is the one thing that's right," Jack contradicted, reaching for her. "Now that this charade of yours is over, we can be together just like we should've been years ago—"

Lisa took a step backwards to evade his grasp. She couldn't stand it if he touched her again. She'd be lost.

"We're not staying married. We're not going to be together. Not now. Not ever. I'm going ahead with the divorce."

Jack's arms dropped to his sides. He stared at her for a few moments, his brows puckered in an uncomprehending frown as if he didn't understand the words. "You're what?"

Lisa shook her head. "You heard me. Nothing has changed."

Jack looked like he'd just been doused with ice water. "What are you talking about? You can't still go through with the divorce. Not now."

"Jack..." Lisa began. She fixed her gaze on the framed photograph of her parents on the dresser behind him, thinking that would be safer than looking at his face.

Jack turned and slammed his fist into the wall. "I don't believe this. Are you out of your mind? You love me. You know you do. And I love you. So what kind of game are you playing?"

Yes, she loved him. The feelings he'd ignited in her almost a dozen years ago were just as strong, just as deep as they were then. She loved him deeply, irrevocably. But she couldn't take the chance that he would leave her again. If he did, she would never survive the pain.

"It's no game, Jack. And you're right. I do love you. I suppose I always have, and I always will. But we're not married. We never really were. Oh, the marriage license said I was your wife, and yes, we consummated the marriage, but you were never my husband. Not really."

"So will it make you feel good to throw me away so that I'll know what it feels like to be dumped."

Lisa's eyes flashed. "I didn't think—"

"That's an understatement."

"I don't expect you to understand—"

"That's a good thing, because I don't. I don't understand at all."

"I can't go through this again. You almost destroyed

me once. I can't let you do that again. Next time I wouldn't survive it."

"This is insane."

"No, Jack," Lisa said quietly, "what's insane is that you think I can forget about what you did to me. You enticed me into your bed, filling me full of hopes and dreams for our future together, then you disappeared out of my life because Daddy tightened the purse strings—"

"I explained all that," Jack protested.

A bitter smile crossed Lisa's face. "Yes, you did. You explained *your* feelings, what *you* thought was the right thing to do, what *you* thought would be best for me. Did it ever occur to you to ask *me*? You left me, without giving me any say in the matter, and I had to pick up the pieces and put my life back together."

"What do you want me to do? How can I convince you that I'm sorry—"

"Then you suddenly show up on my doorstep professing your love for me," she went on, all the hurt and bitterness she'd fought for so long to overcome bubbling to the surface, "and you expect me to throw away everything I've worked for. For what, Jack? So that when the novelty wears off, you can do the same thing to me again?"

"That wouldn't—"

Lisa raised her hand in protest. "Please, spare me the false promises. I won't take that chance again, Jack. You're a user. You use people for what you need, then throw them away like yesterday's newspaper. You used your parents, you used me, you even used Mrs. Randolph to get a ticket to the fund-raiser."

Surprise registered on Jack's face.

"Yes," Lisa went on, almost enjoying Jack's discomfiture. "I know all about your telephone call. I heard all about your *generosity* from Mrs. Randolph," she told him. "Don't worry, I didn't point out your ulterior motives."

Jack opened his mouth to defend himself, but Lisa went on before he could deny her accusations. "I have a good life. I'm happy, or at least I was until you showed up and ruined everything. I had a man I could count on, a career—"

"I hate to tell you this sweetheart, but your career is in the toilet. You should be thanking me for getting you out before it gets flushed. Unless the Randolphs do something drastic in the very near future, every one of their hotels are going to be in receivership within the year."

Lisa's eyes narrowed. She watched his face for a sign that he was lying. He returned her gaze steadily. No tell-tale twitch in his jaw. "You're lying," she accused anyway.

"I wish I was, for your sake. Haven't the creditors been banging on the door?"

"Well, there have been some difficulties...but—"

"And the bank?"

Lisa had to admit that there had been several meetings with executives from the bank holding the mortgages on both Miami hotels. "The bank was threatening to foreclose, but Carter assured me that there was nothing to worry about."

"He did, did he?"

Lisa nodded.

"And you believed him, didn't you?"

"Why should he lie to me?"

"Because he's the captain of a sinking ship, and he doesn't want his crew bailing out on him before he's ready. Have you seen the books lately?"

"Well...no..."

"And what about the rest of the family? Haven't you noticed that they've been more involved than usual for the past few months?"

"I suppose so ..."

"Have you been living on another planet or what? What do you think the family has been doing all that time? Planning a family barbecue? Either they make the hotel a public company and sell shares on the open market, or it's going into bankruptcy. Chances are either way, you're out the door."

Could Jack be telling the truth about the hotel's financial picture? And if he was, why wasn't she aware of how serious the difficulties were? After all, until a few hours ago, she'd planned to be in charge of the entire hotel. Yet, now that Jack had mentioned it, whenever she had even asked for access to the financial records of the hotel, she had been thwarted, not only by the head of the accounting department, but by Carter himself.

"How do you know all this?" she asked suspiciously. Where was Jack getting his information? And why was he so interested in what was going on in the Randolph organization?

"It's my business to know what's going on," he replied stonily. "When the whole Randolph empire crashes down around their ears, I have a client who's waiting to pick up the pieces. I'm glad you aren't going to get buried in the rubble."

For several long moments, neither of them spoke. Finally, Jack broke the silence. "So I guess this is it," he said. "Bye, Lisa. I hope you find what you're looking for."

Then, without another word, he was gone.

Stunned and shaken, she gazed at the door for several moments, almost expecting him to change his mind, to hear his now-familiar knock at the door. Then, when she heard the sound of the elevator fade, tears she had held back flowed freely down her cheeks.

Was she a fool to let Jack walk out of her life? Were her motives selfish? Suddenly, she wasn't so sure.

As she went through her usual night time routine and climbed into bed, the questions swirled through her mind. Questions that had no answers.

It had been three days, and Lisa hadn't heard from Jack once. She hadn't been able to sleep properly since he left, and spent most nights in the stuffed recliner in the living room.

She was still curled up in the chair when Tyler shuffled into the room just after dawn. His hair was tousled, and his cheeks were pink. His eyes were barely open, but he crossed the room and climbed up into Lisa's lap and threw his chubby arms around her neck. He didn't say a word, just wriggled into a comfortable position and nudged his head onto her shoulder.

He stayed like that for several minutes. Lisa thought he must have fallen back to sleep, but finally, he lifted his head and looked into her eyes. "How come your eyes are all red?" he asked innocently. "Were you crying?"

Lisa hugged the little boy close to her, feeling the silkiness of his hair on her cheek. She smiled softly. "Why would I be crying?"

Tyler shrugged. "'Cause you're sad 'cause Jack went away."

How did he know—" Of course, he must have heard them arguing.

"Does that mean he isn't gonna be our uncle?" Tyler persisted.

Hot tears stung Lisa's eyelids, and she looked outside to the dismal morning beyond her apartment. "I don't know," she said softly.

"He said he was gonna be our uncle, and we could go to the water park again, and—"

"He did, did he?" So that's what he'd been doing when he was tucking the boys into bed the night before. Campaigning.

"You must be starving." Lisa couldn't bear to think of all the things they wouldn't be doing together. She lifted the child off her lap and set him steadily on the floor. "What would you like for breakfast? Pancakes? Eggs?"

"Pancakes," Tyler raced into the kitchen, Jack forgotten, at least for the moment. "With oodles and oodles of butter and syrup."

"Again?"

His head bobbed. "I want pancakes every day."

Lisa chuckled. "Not every day, but you can have them today. Now while I'm mixing up the batter, go and get Kevin out of bed and start getting dressed. I don't want you to be late for school or your parents won't let you stay with me again. Now scoot."

FIFTEEN

A soft thud outside the front door drew Lisa's attention. "Kevin," Lisa called from the kitchen, "is that the morning newspaper I hear?"

"I dunno," he called back. "I'll look."

Darn, she thought, she should have waited until Kevin was ready for school before she let him loose with the comic strips. She knew how he tore the newspaper apart at home to get at them as soon as it came in the door.

"Kevin," she called again, "leave the comics until you're dressed."

Silence.

"Kevin?"

Seconds later, she heard his footsteps heading towards the kitchen. He appeared in the doorway, a confused expression on his face, one page of the newspaper crumpled in his fist.

"Aunti Li," he said, holding the newspaper out to her. "How come your picture's in the paper?"

Lisa glanced up from the griddle. She smiled. "Pardon me?"

"There's a picture of you in the paper. And Jack. And the other man."

Lisa's brows knitted in a frown. What was he talking about?

Turning towards him, she laid the spatula on the counter and took the newspaper from his outstretched hand. She uncrumpled it, her gaze focussing on Bebe Karston's gossip column. "Oh…this is not good," she whispered, her eyes skimming the headline.

Lisa gasped, feeling as if someone had physically punched her in the stomach. The headline read "Love Triangle". There were three photographs arranged in a triangle formation. In the photo at the peak of the triangle, Carter and Jack were shaking hands. The caption read "Is husband #1 congratulating husband #2, or is it the traditional handshake between two opponents before the battle?"

In the other two corners of the triangle were photographs of Lisa, one smiling at Carter, the other an almost identical pose, except that it was Jack she was smiling at.

The article continued, dragging up every detail of her marriage to Jack and her engagement to Carter. The knots in Lisa's stomach tightened, and she choked back a wave of nausea as she read the column. How had Bebe Karston found out? Jack. It had to be Jack.

Fury replaced the sick feeling in Lisa's stomach.

How could he do this to her? The betrayal made her feel physically ill. He supposedly loved her, but he'd deliberately chosen to destroy not only her career, but her reputation as well.

"Auntie Li?" Tyler said softly, breaking into Lisa's thoughts. "What's the matter?"

Lisa gazed down at the little boy eyeing her so curiously. She certainly wasn't going to show that she was upset by the article. "Nothing, Kevin. Nothing at all."

"Why's your picture in there?"

"Because ..." Think fast, she told herself. "Because we were all at a party the other night, that's all," she lied.

"Hey, Aunti Li," Kevin yelled suddenly. "Look. You're burning the pancakes."

Lisa spun around. Smoke spiralled in thick coils upwards from the skillet.

From a jukebox in the corner of the Down Home Bar & Grill, Alan Jackson's hit, *Remember When,* filled the room. Whoever had picked it couldn't have done a better job, since that's all Jack seemed to be doing these days.

Most of the stools at the long counter running the length of the bar were empty, not unusual on an early Sunday afternoon. Just him at one end and elderly couple holding hands near the far side of the bar.

Yeah, Jack thought as drained yet another bottle of beer. Me too. Remembering when he and Lisa were a couple, when they thought their love would last forever.

And what good did it do? Considering he was usually fairly intelligent, for the past few weeks he'd been acting like a lovesick teenager. And for what?

So she could get revenge. She wanted to pay him back for the way he'd treated her so many years ago.

Jack held up the empty bottle and waved it in the direction of the bored-looking bartender pouring peanuts into small bowls. Within seconds, a full open bottle appeared in front of him. Jack reached into his pocket and pulled out a set of keys and slid them across the bar. The bartender's brows lifted as he sent Jack a questioning glance, Jack smiled wryly, "I'm planning to be in no condition to use these, so if you wouldn't mind holding on to them for me in case I get stupid and think I'm sober enough to drive..."

The bartender nodded and slipped the key ring into a drawer behind him.

"Keep 'em coming, will you?"

"Sure thing, pal. You want to leave your address so I can put you in a cab when you're ready to leave?"

The bartender offered his pen, and Jack scribbled his address on a napkin.

"I'll be in that booth in the corner," Jack said, picking up his beer and moving toward one of the imitation-leather booths along the grease and dust-covered windows.

He slid into the seat and lifted the bottle to his mouth, feeling the burn as the liquid slid down his throat.

If he was lucky, in a couple of hours, he'd pass out, and the pain would disappear, at least for a while. He couldn't do this regularly, because he didn't like the taste of liquor or beer enough to become an alcoholic, but just for today...

Then he'd decide what to do.

Lisa hung up the telephone and went into the bathroom. Lordy, she thought with a grimace as she glanced at her reflection in the mirror, I hope I sounded better on the phone than I look.

Karen had called to let her know she would be picking up the twins in a few minutes. The twins. Having Tyler and Kevin had been the only bright spot in the past few days, the only thing that had kept her going. And now they would be gone, at least temporarily. If Karen and Larry decided to move away, she'd lose them too.

Tears welled up in her eyes, and she shook her head. Stop it, she admonished herself. Pity parties don't fix anything. If they did, she would have managed to arrange world peace by now.

Quickly, she washed her face and slipped a clean tank top over her head before she ran a brush through her hair. She didn't usually wear makeup at home, but today, she definitely needed something to hide the pallor of her skin and the lack of sparkle in her eyes. A quick swipe of blush and a touch of lip gloss helped somewhat, although she would have had to use a whole bottle of concealer to get rid of the dark shadows around her eyes.

Karen's voice had sounded strained on the telephone. Lisa had hoped that by going away with Larry for a few days, and finding out more about the business, that she'd be able to make the right decision. By the tone of her voice, that hadn't happened.

So now not only her life was in shambles, it seemed Karen's was as well.

Lisa filled the sugar bowl to the brim. If she was right, Karen was going to need it.

She sighed. Only a few weeks ago, she had a career, a fiancé, and a family she knew would always be there for her. Now, she was unemployed, unengaged, and would quite possibly be living alone in the city with no family nearby at all.

Here we go again, she thought as a solitary tear threatened to slip down her cheek. She had to get a grip on herself before Karen arrived. By the subdued tone of her voice on the phone, Lisa knew that Karen would need her. Since she'd been away, Karen probably hadn't heard about the changes at the hotel and her own downfall. Lisa intended to keep it that way. She couldn't let Karen see how upset she was. It sounded as if her sister had enough problems of her own to deal with.

Fifteen minutes later, Lisa heard a knock at the door. When she opened it, she couldn't prevent a small gasp. Karen looked like Lisa felt, and Lisa thought wryly of the turn their lives had taken in such a short time.

Noticing the shadows under her sister's eyes, Lisa laid a gentle hand on Karen's arm. "How did it go?"

Karen shrugged.

Lisa opened her mouth to ask for details, but the din arising from the guest room drowned out her words. Suddenly, the door flew open and the twins burst into the room, squealing with delight when they saw their mother in the foyer.

Hugs, kisses and little boys' voices straining to be heard eliminated the opportunity to speak to Karen. Yet Lisa sensed that Karen needed to talk. "I'll be home all night," she said. I'll probably be home for the rest of my life, she could have added, but restrained herself.

Karen glanced away from the drawing Tyler had shoved into her hand and nodded with understanding. "I'll take the boys home now."

Herding the boys and their belongings together, the boys hugged Lisa after promises they could come and stay with her again. A few minutes later, they were gone.

The silence was overwhelming, but Lisa had barely had time for a quick shower before Karen was back. "I left the boys with Larry," she said. "Got any cookies?"

Oh no, Lisa thought, things must be worse than she thought. Some people might turn to alcohol or cigarettes to relieve stress, but Karen turned to sweets, cookies in particular.

While Karen slumped into the corner of the sofa in Lisa's living room, Lisa rummaged through the kitchen cabinets until she found an unopened bag of cream cookies. Not bothering to put them on a plate, she took the bag into the living room.

She handed the bag to Karen and sank to the sofa beside her.

Karen muttered a quick 'thanks' and dug into it. Only after she'd eaten three and had taken her fourth from the bag did she look up. She ran her finger along the edge of the cookie before she split the two outer biscuits and licked at the filling. Lisa smiled. That was one of Karen's habits she'd had since they were little girls. She'd never been able to eat a cookie without eating the center first.

Finally, Lisa couldn't stand the wait any longer. "So?" she asked, hoping that only that one word would prompt Karen.

Obviously she'd have to pry the information out of her. "What happened at the lake?"

"It was beautiful," she replied grudgingly.

Not exactly the response she'd expected. So what was the problem?

"There's a cute little bungalow that would be ours, the business is very profitable from what I've heard..."

"And?" Lisa prodded.

"And it's everything Larry's ever dreamed of."

To Lisa, it seemed as if Karen should be at home packing instead of sitting in her sister's living room binging on sugar.

"It sounds wonderful."

"It is."

"So why do you look as if it's the end of the world?"

"I told him I wouldn't go, and now I'm afraid it'll be

the end of our marriage. If I stop him, he'll grow to resent me for holding him back." Tears brimmed her eyes, and she wiped them away with the back of her hand.

Now Lisa was completely confused. Their dreams were within reach, and she was pushing them away. "What happened up there?"

"Larry wants this so badly, Lisa. But I can't go with him. I can't take the risk." She lowered her head and started to demolish another cookie.

"Keep this up, by the time you're finished, you'll be too wide to get through the door to go home," Lisa pointed out.

They both laughed, but there was no real mirth.

"Why can't you take the risk?" Lisa asked. "It sounds as if it's the answer to all your prayers."

Karen raised her eyes to meet Lisa's. "I thought you of all people would understand."

She'd like to, Lisa thought. But she didn't.

"After what we went through when we were kids—"

"We aren't kids now and—"

"I know that," Karen burst in, "but what if it doesn't work out? What if we lose everything? Right now Larry has a job, we have a home, we're just starting to put a few extra dollars aside for the future. What if we have to start all over again?"

"You're young—"

"Don't you remember how people treated us because we didn't have any money? I can't go through that again."

Why did Karen's words sound so familiar? Hadn't

she used those same words to Jack just a few days ago? Not the money part, but the fear of taking a chance in case she failed.

"You don't know that it won't work out," Lisa insisted. She had to make Karen realize that she had to take the risk. If she didn't, she might regret it for the rest of her life.

"No, I don't," Karen admitted.

"Do you think Larry would be so anxious to do this if he didn't think he could make a good life for you and the boys there?"

Karen's glance shot up to Lisa. "Of course not."

Lisa smiled at her sister and gently squeezed her free hand. "There's your answer."

A weak smile crossed Karen's face. "Gosh, Lisa. You're right. Larry would never hurt us. All I have to do is to trust him."

The cookie dropped unheeded to the plate as Karen threw her arms around Lisa's neck and hugged her tightly. "Thanks, Lisa. I knew I could count on you."

If only her own problems could be so easily solved, Lisa thought while Karen went into the kitchen to boil water for tea.

"Gosh, I can't believe how selfish I've been, rambling on and on about my problems," Karen called from the kitchen. "I'd almost forgotten about Jack. What was he doing here? What's been going on that you've been keeping secret?"

Karen appeared in the doorway with two cups of steaming tea and put them on the coffee table. While she poured sugar and milk into each of the cups, Lisa told her the entire story.

Karen's mouth was hanging open by the time Lisa finished. "Wow", was all she could say.

Lisa took a sip of the tea. "So that's the end of it," she said with a shrug, noticing how her voice was beginning to break with emotion. "He's gone."

For several seconds, they sat face to face, Karen's gaze locked firmly on Lisa. "Are you crazy?" she asked finally, the tone of her voice implying that Lisa most certainly was.

Lisa's eyebrows drew together in a frown. It wasn't like Karen to raise her voice. "What? Why are you yelling?"

"Because I can't believe what I'm hearing. You've obviously lost your mind."

"What—?"

"You let the only man you've ever loved walk out the door."

Lisa nodded, too miserable to answer. Having Karen put into words exactly what she'd been thinking only made it more painful.

"You do still love him, don't you?" she asked.

Lisa nodded. "I've loved him since the first second I saw him," she murmured sadly.

"He loves you. And you love him. I really don't understand why you're fighting it."

Lisa got up and moved to the window. The moon was full and rode high in the sky. A young couple holding hands strolled by, their laughter filtering through the window. Another couple sat on the bench at the entrance to the park across the street, their arms entwined. It seemed to be a night for lovers. Even the dogs were paired up, she noticed, as two Labrador puppies romped playfully in the park.

What was the problem? How could she explain her fear to Karen?

"It's because he hurt you once before, isn't it?"

Lisa turned back toward Karen, not bothering to hide the tears that welled up in her eyes. "I'm too afraid to risk the pain again."

"You don't know that he'll hurt you again."

"I don't know that he won't."

"You want guarantees? There aren't any."

"I know that. But what if—?"

"You can play 'what-if' until you're old and gray, and it'll never get you anywhere."

"You're right, I suppose..."

Karen sighed. "We make a good pair, don't we?" She smiled grimly. "We're both cowards."

Lisa returned her sister's smile. "We are, aren't we?"

Karen rested her hand on Lisa's arm. "Did you bother to listen to what you told me a few minutes ago?"

"Huh?"

Karen shook her head in exasperation. "What advice did you just give me?"

Lisa shook her head, recalling their earlier conversation. "It's not the same thing at all."

"Of course it is," Karen insisted. "We're both afraid of what might happen, what might not happen, what could happen. Neither one of us can control the future.

You told me to take the chance. I'm telling you to do the same."

Lisa took in a sharp breath. Karen was right. She was a coward. She was so afraid that one day Jack might hurt her again that she was willing to give him up rather than risk it. She'd spent so much time worrying about what might happen that she'd given up her chance at happiness.

She'd been such a fool.

Was it too late? Would Jack still want her if she went to him now, or would he send her away? This was a chance she was willing to take.

Lisa gave her sister a quick hug and crossed to the closet in the foyer. "I have to see him," she said as she jammed her arms into her jacket. "I have to tell him how wrong I was."

A huge grin appeared on Karen's face. "Looks like we're both braver already," she said.

As Lisa opened the door and raced down the corridor to the elevator, she heard her sister's voice. "Sure, I'll let myself out."

SIXTEEN

"I'm sorry, miss, but I can't let you go up to Mr. Brennan's apartment." The security guard, a man who wouldn't have looked out of place in a wrestling ring, blocked her entrance. "He left strict instructions that he didn't want visitors."

"But you have to. I have to speak to him."

"Nobody's going up there until I get orders."

Lisa had been arguing with the guard for the past ten minutes, and she was no closer to seeing Jack than she had been when she'd hurried out of her apartment. There had been an accident on the freeway and traffic had been backed up, making what was normally a fifteen minute drive take well over an hour. And for what? An overdeveloped Neanderthal refusing to listen to her.

She could have called him. She realized that. But would he have listened to her on the phone? She wasn't sure, and wasn't going to take the chance that he'd hang up. She was pretty sure that if she standing at his door, he wouldn't slam it in her face.

Maybe she should go home and try again later. Almost as soon as the thought sprang into her mind, she threw it aside. She'd let him go once before, and she was not letting him go again, even if she had to sit in the lobby for the next three days waiting until he left his apartment.

Unwelcome tears trickled down her cheeks. Angry at herself for allowing a stranger to see her fall apart, she yanked her purse from her shoulder and began to dig through it for a tissue.

The guard's voice suddenly gentled, and he pulled a tissue from a box on the console. "Now, now," he murmured. "Oh, jeez, don't start crying. What is it with you women? Jeez, I can't stand it when women cry. My wife did that the other night just 'cause I brought her a little bunch of flowers."

So the guard standing between her and Jack wasn't the caveman she'd first taken him for. He had a weak spot after all.

Lisa sniffed loudly. "Was it a special occasion?" she asked.

"Naw," he muttered, his beefy face taking on a pinkish glow. "I sometimes get to feeling a little guilty that I don't spend much time with her and the kids, so I thought she'd like them. I didn't think she'd bawl for half an hour."

So he had a romantic streak, too. Maybe...just maybe if she told him the truth...What the heck, she decided. At this point, it couldn't hurt.

All she had to do was think about the future without Jack, and tears welled up in her eyes and spilled over. Haltingly, she sputtered out the truth. Almost instantly, the guard's expression changed. His eyes gazed at her sympathetically, and he gently patted her arm when she was finished.

"Oh, jeez, I don't know. I mean, I feel sorry for you, but it's my job to make sure...oh, jeez ..."

"I understand," Lisa whimpered. "It's just that..."

She glanced up at him, giving him the most pitiful glance she could muster. It obviously had the right effect, because he muttered a few words under his breath. Finally, to her he said "Go," and pointed to the bank of elevators as he turned his back and suddenly became very interested in something going on outside.

Impulsively, Lisa reached up and brushed her lips on his cheek. "Thank you," she whispered.

A minute later, she stood in front of Jack's door. Her hands trembled. Her heart pounded erratically. What if he sends me away? What if he's decided I'm not worth the trouble? What if—?"

Stop it, she scolded herself. Stop playing 'what if'. 'What if' had caused most of the problems she had now, and she made a promise to herself right then and there that she would never play that game again.

With a shaky hand, she knocked on Jack's door. She waited. Nothing. She knocked again, louder this time. Still nothing. She knew he was inside, so why wasn't he answering? Had the security guard had second thoughts about letting her in? Had he warned Jack that she was on her way and he didn't want to see her? That must be it, she decided. She'd lost him. By worrying about what might happen one day in the future, she had lost the only future she'd ever really wanted.

With her tears now streaming freely down her cheeks, she turned away from the door and trudged slowly down the corridor toward the elevators. She punched in the button and slumped against the wall. Once and for all, it was over. She'd let him go again without fighting for what she wanted. And now she would have to live with the consequences.

She heard a door open, but didn't even glance up. "What do you want?" a deep male voice boomed, echoing in the empty corridor.

Lisa started, the shock making her heart bounce. She turned toward the voice. Jack stood in his open doorway. Her heart fluttered with hope that he hadn't been ignoring her, while at the same time she realized he was very angry.

Stubble shadowed his chin, and his hair was tousled as if he'd been sleeping. His eyes were dark, filled with pain.

All he wore was a pair of faded denim jeans, and Lisa couldn't control the tingle that swept through her at the sight of his naked chest. For an instant, she wondered if she'd always feel that way whenever she looked at him.

She took a hesitant step towards him. Then another.

He didn't move.

Finally, they were only inches apart. "You've been

drinking," she said, noticing the odor of alcohol. "You never drink."

"You make me do a lot of things I don't normally do," he replied.

"Oh."

Now that she was face to face with him, she had no idea what to say, how to explain to him what she'd learned, how to make him understand.

"What are you doing here, Lisa?" he asked after a few moments.

She wanted nothing more than to throw herself into his arms, but she wouldn't. At least not until she'd said what she came to say, and she was sure he wouldn't reject her.

She took a deep breath and lifted her eyes to look directly at him. If he turned her away this time, she was determined it wasn't going to be because he didn't know how she felt. She'd accused him of not allowing her to be part of the decision when they'd separated before. That wasn't going to happen again.

"I..." She paused, searching for the right words.

"Yes?"

Okay, girl, spit it out. "I made a mistake. I was wrong. I love you and I want to spend the rest of my life with you."

Jack glanced at her suspiciously. "What? Say that again?"

Lisa repeated the words.

"I thought that's what you said."

"I was afraid to take the chance of loving you again."

"And you aren't now?" he asked, his words filled with doubt. "What changed your mind?"

Lisa shook her head. "It's all thanks to Karen." She let out a short laugh. "Funny story. I gave her some advice and she threw it back at me. It was then I realized that life is about taking risks, that if I don't take the chance of losing you one day, I've lost you anyway. So, there's no decision to make. Any time I have with you is better than nothing."

Jack reached up and cupped her chin in his palm, stroking her cheek with his thumb. That simple movement was all she needed.

She would always carry the fear deep in her heart that he would leave her again, but she wouldn't allow that fear to cloud the happiness they could have together. If it was meant to be, they would spend the rest of their lives together, raise a family together, grow old together. She'd be a fool to turn her back on that.

"You're sure?"

"Positive."

Suddenly, Lisa felt herself being drawn into the tight circle of his arms. "I've never wanted anyone but you," he whispered, his lips grazing her ear.

"I'm glad."

"The divorce—"

"I'll call my attorney first thing in the morning."

"So you still want to be my wife?"

His wife. The word had a wonderful ring to it. Lisa looked up at him and nodded. She wanted nothing more.

"We wasted so many years."

She gazed up at him, all the love inside shining in her eyes. He kissed her then, and when he finally released her, she grinned. "You're right. We have a lot of time to make up for. I shouldn't have let you go, but you know what they say."

"What's that?"

"Better late than never."

ABOUT THE AUTHOR

Lauryn Alexander writes heartwarming stories of families, friendships and romance. Although she lives in Canada, she is a beach-lover at heart and spends as much time as possible in the sunny south. When she's not writing, you can usually find her wielding a pool cue or a pair of knitting needles.

Website: www.laurynalexander.com
Newsletter: www.laurynalexander.com/newsletter
Facebook: www.facebook.com/laurynalexanderbooks